How t

Ellie wanted [illegible] herself, just to see if she was dreaming. Her innards may have melted to blissful mush, but something wasn't right here.

She'd just cried all over Daniel Morgan's shirt. Where Daniel's caress had scared her witless on the beach the other night, tonight it somehow liberated her. She felt lighter.

And that kiss! Admittedly she'd been waiting for him to kiss her since that night on the beach. She'd wondered what Daniel's kiss would be like, even fantasized about it. Tonight she learned it was all that fantasy and more.

But whatever was going on here, it wasn't going any further. She had her life planned, thank you very much, and it didn't include danger with a capital Daniel.

Dear Reader,

What does romance mean to you? Sure, it could be sharing a candlelit dinner or strolling hand in hand on a spring day. But to me it's even the smallest of gestures that tells you the person you think hangs the sun and the moon finds you equally unforgettable. As a lifelong romantic who met her future husband nearly twenty years ago, I'm delighted to be heading up Silhouette Romance. These books remind me that no matter what challenges the day has held, finding true love is one of life's greatest rewards.

Bestselling author Judy Christenberry kicks off another great month with *Finding a Family* (SR #1762). In this sweet romance, a down-to-earth cowboy goes "shopping" for the perfect woman for his father but instead finds himself the target of Cupid's arrow! Watch the sparks fly in Melissa McClone's *Blueprint for a Wedding* (SR #1763) when a man who has crafted the perfect blueprint for domestic bliss finds himself attracted to an actress who doesn't believe in happy endings. This month's "Cinderella" is a feisty Latina, as Angie Ray continues Silhouette Romance's commitment to offering modern-day fairy tales in *The Millionaire's Reward* (SR #1764). Part of the SOULMATES series, *Moonlight Magic* (SR #1765) by Doris Rangel features a vacationing nurse who falls for a handsome stranger with a particularly vexing habit of vanishing into thin air.

And be sure to stay tuned for next month's exciting lineup when reader favorites Raye Morgan and Carol Grace return with two classic romances.

Ann Leslie Tuttle
Associate Senior Editor

Moonlight Magic

DORIS RANGEL

Soulmates

Published by Silhouette Books
America's Publisher of Contemporary Romance

For J and A
Who created their own Hawaiian Magic
With love from Mom
and Grammie

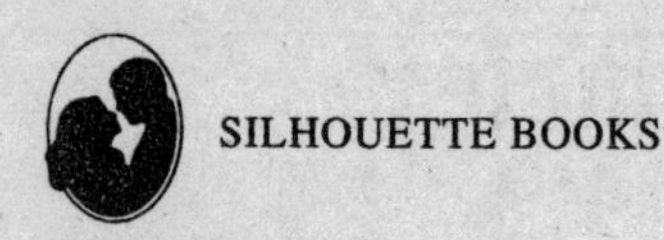

ISBN 0-373-19765-9

MOONLIGHT MAGIC

This edition published by arrangement with Harlequin Books S.A.

Visit Silhouette Books at www.eHarlequin.com

Printed in U.S.A.

Books by Doris Rangel

Silhouette Romance

Marlie's Mystery Man #1693
Moonlight Magic #1765

Silhouette Special Edition

Mountain Man #1140
Prenuptial Agreement #1224

DORIS RANGEL

loves books—the feel of them, the sight of them, the smell of them. And she loves talking about them. She has collected them, organized them, sold them new and used, written them, worked with others to write them, read them aloud to children and has hopefully imparted the magic of them to the grade school, college and adult students she has taught over the years. History, philosophy, science, satire, Western, mystery... In her home, books are the wallpaper of choice.

Romances hold a special place on her shelves, however. A story that ends with a couple stepping into the future with love and hope may be an ideal, but it is an ideal she wishes in the tomorrows of every living thing in the universe. Love, after all, in whatever form it takes, is all that is.

Prologue

Daniel Morgan startled into wakefulness.

But around him quiet reigned in the garden's somnambulant midafternoon sunshine—as it should with the children in school, Janie and Tom at work, and the old woman in the house probably watching afternoon soaps.

Yet he'd felt someone touch him, brush warm fingers across his chest.

Dreaming again.

Idly, he listened to the breeze rustling quietly through the foliage and watched an insect investigate the heart of a nearby blossom.

Thoughts drifting to other times, other places, he sank again into lethargy...and slept.

* * *

If you can't trust your sweet, old grandmother, who can you trust?

Running the tip of her finger over a silver petal on the earring she held, Ellie frowned. She trusted Grammie. Sure she did.

Most of the time.

The pair of earrings *looked* ordinary enough. Flower shaped, with a slight dangle from a French hook and attached to an ordinary flat plastic backing stamped, Plumeria, the Flower of Hawaii and Sterling Silver. The backing nestled on ordinary cotton batting in a small ordinary white cardboard box with Made especially for you by Ohana embossed on the lid. Shops used this kind of box by the thousands.

Grammie's gift was perfectly...well, ordinary. A nice pair of unpretentious earrings, not terribly expensive, their shape the only exotic thing about them.

"Nice."

Looking up, Ellie found the flight attendant standing beside her admiring the earrings.

"Thanks. They're a gift from my grandmother," Ellie told her. And that was an ordinary comment—if one didn't know her grandmother.

She shivered.

"They're very pretty. Is this your first trip to the islands?" the woman asked casually, pouring the soda Ellie requested.

"Yes. I'm going for a medical convention, but my brother is a marine stationed there so I'm visiting him, too."

Inwardly, Ellie grimaced, knowing she'd given the flight attendant far more information than the polite question warranted. She wasn't usually this chatty, but for some reason she was nervous. The earrings, probably.

"I'm sure you'll have a wonderful time," the woman replied, and passed on to the next passenger.

I certainly hope so. Ellie's dubious gaze dropped again to the silver flower in her hand.

Did Grammie really *buy these earrings?*

The Simms family had a good-natured saying among themselves: Never trust one of Grammie's little gifts if she didn't buy it.

Their grandmother, descended from an Iq'nata shaman, had a stash of seemingly ordinary personal items that, if she decided to give one of them to you, had a way of bringing about all sorts of extraordinary events.

Not bad events, just strange ones.

Over the years the family had learned to politely refuse any items for which Gram hadn't paid cold, hard cash. Grammie never took it personally. She just laughed, told them they had no sense of adventure and pulled out something obviously store-bought as their gift instead.

Right before leaving to catch her flight, Ellie had declined Grammie's first "little something for your trip, dear"—a lei of pretty speckled shells her grandmother said she'd found on the beach when she traveled to Hawaii several years before.

Uh-oh.

When Ellie shook her head decisively, Gram smiled, her blue eyes twinkling with mischief.

"Just teasing, darling. But here's something I know you'll want," and she gave Ellie the box containing the earrings. "I searched the shops for days before I discovered them in a little out-of-the-way place outside of Honolulu."

At Ellie's narrow-eyed look, the older woman lifted an eyebrow. "Don't be so suspicious, Ellie. It's a bad habit of yours." Tilting the box so the light gleamed off the silver flowers, Gram smiled. "Aren't they pretty? They'll look perfect with your sarong."

"I don't have a sarong," Ellie replied.

But she accepted the earrings. They *were* pretty. So…islandish.

Now, rehooking the earring to the plastic backing, she returned the set to the box and dropped it into her purse, dismissing her suspicions.

Not until she'd maneuvered her way to the exit with the rest of the disembarking passengers did Ellie remember another Simms family saying….

The Great Ones have a weird sense of humor.

Chapter One

From his place among the hibiscus, Daniel watched the party eddy around him. The old woman, bless her, never forgot him on occasions such as this. Several leis, many of them made with plumeria blossoms, hung about his neck.

He loved family get-togethers and already felt a little drunk on the heady scent of flowers mixed with the equally heady odor of barbecue.

Being physically sober as a post, it was an inebriation of the senses only, of course. What he wouldn't give for a plate heaped high with food and a frosty cup of beer to wash it down.

Unfortunately, he was only a bystander at this luau. Literally. In the midst of jubilation, Daniel stood apart, watching it all.

Though an adult party—Tom had turned forty—children were everywhere, chasing each other, dodging groups of adults, giggling, shouting. At home, children wouldn't be allowed at a function such as this, Daniel mused, but in Hawaii *ohana* prevailed. He loved it.

The adults, too, milled about, teasing, laughing, talking, sidestepping children sometimes or absently scooping up a young one to cuddle a moment before sending the child off to play again.

And music flowed through it all, everything from Elvis at his most powerful to Iz at his most fragile.

He'd love to dance again, Daniel thought—jiggle his bones to a jazzy beat, shake his booty and *get down* to rock 'n' roll, press his undulating body against a woman's to the breathy croon of a saxophone....

Maybe all of the above, as various couples were doing on the patio.

Two little girls flung each other about madly while four teenagers, three girls and a boy, hip-hopped to the same music. An elderly man and woman showed they still had it, and a younger woman with long silvery-blond hair swayed in ministeps with a seriously intent boy of about five.

Make that six. When the woman said something, the boy looked up at her with a gap-toothed grin, causing her to laugh.

Over the music and the chattering crowd, Daniel couldn't hear the laugh, but the woman had a killer smile.

Earlier, he'd seen her among the guests and admired her silvery hair that she wore long and loose down her back. Though dressed in a gauzy dress that set off her slim figure, she hadn't impressed him as being particularly pretty; she was even, perhaps, a little austere.

But that smile! It transformed a plain-vanilla exterior into something fascinating and mysterious, as if he'd opened a shoe box and found a piece of exotically carved antique ivory. When she smiled, the woman became breathtakingly beautiful!

And she was coming his way.

The thing winked at her!

Nah, it couldn't have.

Ellie eyed the small statue tucked among the flowers. A tiki god, probably, and obviously old, its wood weathered and cracked in places.

She'd seen similar carvings at the Polynesian Cultural Center when the convention arranged a trip there. But they'd been huge. This one stood only about three feet high.

Around its neck hung several leis, she assumed in honor of the party. Yet something else about it seemed different from the others she'd seen.

The eyes, Ellie realized. The carvings at the Cultural Center didn't have such wide awake eyes...eyes with a glint of mischief in them staring right back at her.

Ellie shook her head. *Get real, woman!*

She was just overtired. Overstimulated.

After working with no letup for the past couple of years, being around so many laughing partying people was tiring—even these gregarious Hawaiians, whose pleasure in the moment seemed to waft as naturally as the light tropical breeze.

Perhaps sensing this, Georgie, her young dancing partner, had brought her to this relatively secluded spot before leaving to fetch her a soft drink.

Dismissing the carving from her thoughts, Ellie found herself a seat on a low wall bordering the garden to await the child's return.

Lush tropical blossoms perfumed the night, and she closed her eyes the better to enjoy their scent and the music and laughter from the party just beyond. She smiled to herself when she heard her brother's full-bodied laugh.

And just like that, a dark smothering wave of loneliness washed over her.

On a sharp breath Ellie fought it back. This had happened a lot lately, and she was having none of it. She loved her life. She loved her job.

Okay, she needed this vacation. She was tired. Being alone, however, was a choice, not a tragedy.

Prickles shimmied up the back of her neck.... With a small gasp, Ellie's eyes flew open.

Someone stared at her! She could feel their intense gaze. She also felt conspicuous and embarrassed at being observed in what she thought was a private moment.

Scanning the crowd, ready to coolly outstare whoever found her introspection so interesting, she could find no one looking her way, however.

Yet someone's knowing observation kept her awareness on full alert.

Slowly, cautiously, Ellie turned her head...and came nose to nose with the crimson orifice of a hibiscus blossom, its golden pistil thrust forward in the flower version of a raspberry.

Startled, she drew back, only to laugh softly at her own paranoia. The rude hibiscus would pay for its impudence, though. Snapping it from its stem, Ellie hooked it over one ear, her fingers brushing one of her flower-shaped earrings in the process.

No sarong, Grammie, she thought, *but I feel a hula coming on.*

Still smiling, and about to turn away, she again started violently, this time with a small muffled shriek. Nestled among the blossoms and thick foliage, the tiki stared back at her, its carved face a study of violence, its eyes infinitely sad and lonely.

She leaped to her feet.

"Here's your soda, Miss Ellie."

Georgie stood beside her, offering an aluminum can, his face one big beam of gap-toothed smile.

"What? Oh. Uh, thanks, sweetie."

Ellie took the soda gratefully and downed a healthy swig. From the corner of her eye, she checked out the carving.

The thing hadn't moved a muscle, its wooden head still angled toward the spot where she'd been sitting. Only, she wasn't sitting there anymore. The statue's gaze wasn't following her at all.

Time to leave. She'd be a certified basket case if she didn't get back to Chad's apartment and get some rest. Three days of back-to-back workshops at the convention in Honolulu and a busy day since her arrival at her brother's apartment this morning made for one pooped, overimaginative tourist.

After dumping her luggage in his spare bedroom,

Chad immediately whisked her off for a long drive to loop the island. When they returned, she'd played baseball with the kids next door and been invited by them and their grandmother to this party.

Now her busy day—heck, her busy week, busy year, busy decade—had caught up with her. She needed her bed.

When Georgie ran off to play with the other children, Ellie searched for her brother to tell him she was leaving. Chad was never difficult to locate. With his easygoing, always friendly personality, all she had to do was find the group with the most laughter.

Then she looked for her hosts, Janie and Tom Kamehana, to make her goodbyes, and finally went to Nona, the children's grandmother who had invited her to the luau in the first place.

"You're leaving us," Nona said before Ellie could speak. The old woman took Ellie's hand in her own brown one, the clasp warm and strong. "You're tired," she added.

Ellie smiled. "Yes. But I've had a wonderful time. Thank you for inviting me."

"And your brother. All this time living right next door and I didn't realize," Nona said. She tilted her head, smiling wryly. "Careless of me."

There wasn't much Ellie could say to that. The old woman still held her hand.

"How did you like my garden ornament?"

Ellie strove for diplomacy. "Well, it was, uh—"

"Interesting, yes? I saw you looking at it."

"Is it a tiki god?" Ellie asked cautiously, unsure of the manners involved with the direction the conversation had taken.

"I'm not sure," the old woman replied. "A few years ago one of the children found the carving washed up on the beach of the cove and brought it home. I placed it in the garden. But it's different from the usual, wouldn't you say?"

Feeling completely out of her depth, Ellie smiled. Nona still held her hand. "Everything in Hawaii seems different from the usual to me," she answered apologetically. "I'm from Texas."

Nona nodded her head. "San Antonio."

Ellie didn't remember telling her that, but she supposed she had. Or perhaps Chad did.

Finally Nona let go her hand. "You might enjoy a walk on the beach, child. Such a beautiful evening. The moon will be lovely on the water."

"Perhaps I'll do that," Ellie replied politely, having no intention of doing any such thing. All she wanted was her bed and the opportunity to forget about wooden carvings with sad lonely eyes. "Good night."

Nona smiled and picked up the toddler pulling on her skirt and waving a piece of something sticky. "Good night, dear. Those are lovely earrings, by the way. I once had a pair just like them."

Self-consciously Ellie touched an earring, murmured, "Thank you," and added another good-night.

See, she thought. *Ordinary. Mass produced. As Gram says, I'm too suspicious.*

She let herself out the side entrance separating her brother's apartment from the house next door, her overexposed senses relaxing when the closed gate muted the music and laughter, and intervening trees shut out the colored party lights. A three-quarter moon gilded the night with silver.

It was, indeed, a beautiful evening. Too beautiful to go indoors just yet, even though she was tired, Ellie thought. The moonlight *would* be lovely on the water, and she remembered a small, secluded cove only a block away.

Chad had shown it to her earlier. Though native Hawaiians often went there, he said, mainlanders seldom used it, probably because other beaches were bigger, sandier, more picturesque. The waters of the cove were known to be dangerous, too. Signs warned against swimming.

No problem. Ellie didn't plan to swim.

In moments she'd walked down the quiet residential street ending at a stretch of pale sand bordering a moonstruck sea. A dead end leading to paradise.

Only in Hawaii.

Ellie touched one of the silver earrings in her ears and smiled a little as she imagined Grammie's chuckle in the breeze rustling through the trees behind her.

Slipping off her sandals, she stood at the edge of the water and gazed out at the sea before her, its wavelets liquid pearls lapping at her feet.

Bliss.

Nona watched Ellie slip out the side gate.

Interesting, she thought, her gaze swinging to the small carving ruling its hibiscus kingdom across the way. But hibiscus were merely decorative. They had no power. Plumeria, now…

Taking her time, the toddler still riding her ample hip,

Nona strolled over to give the carving a closer inspection. Then, with a low sudden laugh, she whipped the plumeria leis from its neck and placed them around the neck of the child.

There. That ought to do it.

Daniel looked around in disbelief.

The party had disappeared. The music was silent. Heck, the whole back garden was gone. He was…

He was on a beach.

Wait a minute! He was at the *cove!*

White sand shaped like a crescent moon cupping a bump in the Pacific; the oddly shaped tamarisk tree over there…. He knew this place, all right.

Sure enough, some distance away and picked out by bright moonlight, he saw the sign sticking up from the sand. He didn't have to be any closer to know exactly what it said.

DANGER NO SWIMMING STAY OUT OF THE WATER.

The damned thing's too small, he thought bitterly. *And damned near worthless. This place needs an electrified fence around it, not a puny little hand-lettered sign. Twenty-four-hour guard dogs ought to patrol the area, trained to drag people away if they came within a hundred feet of the water.*

Better yet, some civic-minded citizen should fill it in with cement, pave it over and make it a parking lot. The cove's very existence invited tragedy.

What if someone couldn't read that paltry notice—or was too stupid to recognize a warning when they read one?

Scowling at the distant, slightly tilted sign, Daniel angrily forked his fingers through his hair.

And stilled.

Inch by careful inch, he lowered his hand to stare at his fingers, still splayed as they'd been in his hair.

Hair?

Not daring to hope, he reached up again—actually *raised* his arm and hand—and lightly touched the top of his head. Against his palm he felt the crisp pelt of his...hair.

But as he again stared at his hand in awe, a small movement just beyond caught his attention, and Daniel lifted his head sharply. Someone besides himself was on the beach.

A woman, he realized, sitting on the sand, arms clasping her knees as she stared out over the sea. Her hair, the same color as moonlight, lifted slightly in the breeze. The woman from Tom and Janie's party.

And she sat within inches of the water.

Ready to warn her, Daniel took a step, only to become aware of what he'd just done. Looking down at himself, his own wonder captivated him again.

He still wore his boxers, he saw. And...he fought an urge to laugh wildly...his money belt! Had anything else about him changed?

His bare chest and flat stomach looked no leaner, no fuller. His legs were as muscled, as much from walking a thousand miles of hospital corridor as from deliberate exercise. Near the small toe of one bare foot ran the thin line of a scar he'd had since he was twelve.

It was his body all right. His arms, his legs, what he

assumed was his face. Nothing about it was different. And he had *moved!*

The thought brought him back to the present with a thump.

The woman! While he'd been checking himself over, she had risen from her seat on the sand and now swished one foot in the tiny wavelets washing the shore.

"Hey! Don't do that!"

A part of him marveled at the sound of his voice echoing over the beach, but this time Daniel didn't take time to enjoy it. He headed toward the woman at a dead run.

She turned a startled face in his direction, dropped her sandals and ran, too.

Away from him.

Her action stopped Daniel in his tracks.

Women didn't used to run from him. Did he not have his same face after all?

But the silly woman continued running down the beach, her moonlit hair streaming behind her—each frantic step splashing in the shallow water of the shoreline, sometimes at its edge, sometimes a little deeper.

Daniel pelted after her again. Whatever hid in the waters of this cove was dangerous. Stay out of the Water the sign said.

An order, not a warning.

The woman ran like a deer, but in the wrong direction.

She was afraid of him, he guessed, and if she'd just aim toward the trees or toward the houses beyond, he'd leave her alone. He had other things to think about.

But in her panic, she raced down the shoreline, her tracks weaving in and out of the shallow, gently breathing water.

So he tackled her.

Chapter Two

"Oomph!"

Ellie hit the sand, with her assailant landing on top of her. But she hadn't spent two nights a week and a small fortune on self-defense classes for nothing.

As she landed she rolled, and before he could get a grip on her, she lifted her knee and made a dent in the man's chances for future children.

Her aim was off, but good enough to make him fall away from her with a groan.

Leaping to her feet, she took off again.

"Not that way, you idiot!" she heard the man gasp behind her. "Toward the street! Run to the houses!"

And Ellie finally understood what her attacker was trying to tell her.

He was right. Like the idiot he'd called her, she was

running up the beach when escape lay toward the neighborhood just beyond it. Heck, Chad's apartment was only a block away.

Something didn't make sense here.

Still running, but slowing a bit, she risked a look over her shoulder.

Her assailant remained where he'd fallen, only now he was sitting up and hugging his knees tightly, his head drooping.

Ellie jogged in place, considering the situation, then turned fully around to stare at the hunched figure from a safe distance.

Other than waving an arm toward the town behind them, he ignored her.

"Are you all right?" she asked, taking a few steps toward him but ready to speed away again at the least hint she hadn't completely clobbered him.

"Peachy. But at least I know all of me works." He groaned. "Did work."

She took a few more steps in his direction, the better to give him the full effect of her glare. "Take it as a warning the next time you attack a woman," she replied coldly. "Just be glad I didn't connect as well as I should have."

"Oh, I'm glad. Trust me." His bitter laugh checked abruptly. "And I didn't attack you."

"No? Guess we don't read the same dictionary. What do you call chasing a woman so you can knock her down?"

"Ah, you *can* read." The man's forehead still rested on his knees, but his tone matched hers for sarcasm. "So why didn't you? And I call it trying to save your stupid neck."

"Why didn't I what?"

"Read the sign," he growled.

"I did. Since I wasn't swimming, I don't see what the problem is."

At last the man lifted his head so he could gaze at her, his handsome face a study of disgust.

Handsome? The man was drop-dead gorgeous!

"It doesn't just say No Swimming," he bit out. "It says, and this is a direct quote, 'Danger no swimming stay out of the water.' No commas, no periods, no question marks."

"I barely had a foot in it," Ellie replied coldly, then paused. "Are you saying the water is polluted?"

"Of course not. But the water here is dangerous. The sign says so, and I know so. Yet there you were, ignoring the warning like the mainlander you are."

Ellie sighed. Talk about overreaction! But the night was far too beautiful to argue. So what the heck.

With opportunities in short supply for rescuing damsels these days, let the guy have his water dragon.

"All right. I should have paid attention," she conceded, by now standing beside him. "Thanks for your, um, efforts on my behalf. I'm sorry I hurt you."

His smile did weird things to her knees.

"And I'm sorry I frightened you," he said, putting out a hand. "Even?"

Her knees might be weak, but Ellie's brain wasn't. She eyed the out-thrust hand for a long, cautious moment. Still, judging by the lingering pain in the man's eyes, he probably wasn't up to much.

Bending toward him, she, too, extended her hand.

"Even," she said.

As the warm fingers wrapped around hers, the moon came out from behind a cloud and she saw his face clearly.

And liked what she saw.

Movie-star looks honed by an aristocratic bone structure and fine features. A good strong nose set off by an equally strong jaw and wide mobile mouth. Pale hair washed even paler in the moonlight. Eyes…

His eyes looked familiar.

"Have we met?" she asked, finally remembering to withdraw her hand.

Appearing a little unsettled himself, he released it. "Uh, no. I, er, saw you at the party."

"The Kamehanas'? I don't remember seeing you there." She would have remembered.

"There was quite a crowd. You were dancing with a short charmer with a missing front tooth."

Ellie chuckled. Here was another charmer, she'd bet. And after that unexpected moment of traitorous loneliness at the party, she was in the mood to be charmed…to prove to herself that she could be, perhaps, but also because the night simply begged for light flirtation.

Who better than this extremely handsome man to practice on?

She sat down on the sand. "That was Georgie," she told him.

"I know. Another cousin, I hear."

"Really?"

He grinned. "In this case, really, but not always. To Hawaiians, every guest becomes an honorary cousin and is treated like family."

"It's a lovely custom."

They sat silently a moment, listening to the low murmur of the waves brushing the sand a few feet away and to the distant music coming from the neighborhood behind them, probably from the luau they'd both just left.

"Feeling better?" Ellie asked at last.

"Working on it."

Actually, Daniel felt pretty damn good but was afraid the woman might leave if he admitted it. Even though he had a lot to do himself with the business of getting home again, he didn't want to break this up just yet.

After years of silence, just sitting on a beach and talking of nothing much with a pretty girl was a small miracle.

"I know I frightened you," he said tentatively, "but will you tell me your name?"

"Ellie. Yours?"

"Daniel."

"Not Dan or Danny?"

"Only when my mother isn't around."

"My mom tried to make everyone call me Eliza Ann, but she was outnumbered," Ellie replied with a light laugh. "I guess your mom carries more clout."

His answering chuckle delighted his ears. People ought to realize how truly special laughter is to the human race.

"My mother is never outnumbered," he responded, reveling in this wonderful, meaningless conversation.

Yet for a moment he thought about his mother.

Even the disappearance of her only son probably didn't throw Catherine Morgan for long. His mother... she'd certainly never been a "mom"...most likely set up search headquarters in the living room, had her senator call in the FBI, gave everyone drinks and hors d'oeuvres, then took it as a personal affront when her son ruined the party by not being found immediately.

"She sounds formidable."

But Daniel didn't want to talk about his mother. Or himself. After all, what could he say?

"Are you in Hawaii on vacation?" he asked.

Ellie's smile glowed out at him.

With her long silvery hair, and with her face turned up to the night sky, the woman could be mistaken for a moon goddess.

Maybe she was. Daniel stilled. He didn't trust this cove.

But her answer couldn't have been more normal.

"Yes and no. I came for a pediatrics convention in Honolulu, but I have a brother here with the marines. He'll be leaving for Japan soon, so I'm taking the opportunity to spend time with him."

"Pediatrics? You're an M.D.?"

"Pediatric nurse. How about you?"

"Small world. I'm a doctor. Just finished my residency."

All true, but how many years ago? Four? He wasn't sure anymore.

"Oh, were you here for the conference, too?"

"Um, no. So how do you like Hawaii?"

"It's beautiful, what I've seen of it. I haven't had a chance to be a tourist yet, except for a visit to the cultural center."

She wiggled her toes in the sand, and Daniel thought he'd never seen anything so lovely as the shine of pale nail polish on the sweetest feet in the islands.

He smothered an inward grin at this new appreciation of feet. If nothing else, the past years had been a lesson in what to appreciate. Things once taken for granted he now considered in a whole new light. He could hardly wait to go home.

But there was something else he'd learned in the Kamehanas' back garden.

Enjoy the moment.

And at this moment, he was on a beautiful beach—as long as one stayed out of the water—enjoying a beautiful night, talking nothings with a breathtaking woman.

Talking? On a night like this? What was he thinking!

After years of isolation, he wasn't greedy. But a modest little kiss with a moon goddess wouldn't be asking too much, would it? Would Ellie be willing?

Sifting sand through her fingers, Ellie idly watched it catch the breeze, very much aware of being observed.

On a deserted beach with a total stranger, she should be afraid. But fear was the farthest thing from her mind. It was all she could do not to stare back.

Something about Daniel attracted her as she hadn't been attracted in years, though he wasn't her type at all.

Too handsome, for one thing. She'd never been susceptible to handsome men. Fashion-model looks and muscled physiques might be the stuff of most women's fantasies but not hers.

The touch of vulnerability she sensed that had her wanting to reach out to him was another thing. Normally she found vulnerability a turnoff in men because she equated the word with "needy." Her ex-husband sprang to mind.

If you love me, you'll stay home with me. Let someone else take the extra shift.

Ellie shook the memory away. It wasn't that kind of vulnerability she sensed in Daniel. Behind the easy-going charm that said he'd been practicing it for years, she sensed strength in him. And sadness.

She shook that thought away, too.

So what was the attraction? The man was just too perfect for her taste.

Handsome, charming *and* a doctor? Yeah, right. Surely he'd made that last up. What were the odds? Most likely he was the male equivalent to a beach bunny.

Aha! Ellie swallowed the urge to laugh outright. *That* was the attraction.

On a lovely beach on a moonlit night in Hawaii, she'd met the perfect kind of man for her—a studly beach bum. Here now, gone with the tide.

And she'd bet the ranch this particular stud-muffin wanted to kiss her.

She would let him, too, Ellie thought. What fool ignored perfection? And after a kiss or two, she would put on her sandals and return to Chad's apartment.

Alone.

If Daniel found her tomorrow or in the days ahead and wanted to continue where they left off, maybe she would.

Maybe she wouldn't.

It depended on Chad's duty schedule and how much free time he had. Ellie planned to spend as much time as possible with her brother, but when Chad was busy, Daniel might be fun to hang out with. He apparently knew the island well.

Perfect. A vacation flirtation.

Something to laugh about over coffee with her colleagues when she got home.

"Ellie."

Even knowing this scene for exactly what it was, and knowing that Daniel was getting ready to exercise his best come-on, when he said her name like that, low and a little bit rough, Ellie shivered.

Make that sizzled.

"Umm?"

"I..." He cleared his throat. "Uh, where are you from?"

Was that *shyness* she heard? Couldn't be. Didn't fit the image.

"Texas," she said, and slowly turned her head from her study of the sea so that she could look at him.

What she saw made her breath catch. "S-San Antonio," she added in a husky whisper.

"Ah." His gaze never left her mouth. "Would you mind if I kissed you?"

He had to ask? "Please," Ellie managed to breathe. Her eyes fluttered shut.

But it wasn't Daniel's *lips* she felt next.

The stroke of gentle fingers brushing the side of her face took her completely by surprise before their trail down the contours of her jaw lured her into a sensual wonderland.

Warm, firm, but infinitely light, his thumbs traced the slope of her nose and traveled on to outline the fullness of her lower lip.

Her lips parted in a silent plea for more.

"God, you're beautiful," Daniel whispered.

Perhaps he whispered.

By now his light caress had Ellie's senses so adrift she didn't know if he actually spoke. Only her sense of the tactile still operated, working overtime as her body gave birth to nerve endings born singing beneath this man's hands.

His fingers whispered that her skull was perfect, her skin flawless, her facial muscles works of art. Ellie knew she was lovely because those fingers said it.

They twined through her hair, combed slowly through it to its ends, and she understood her hair was a silken glory, a perfection of color and texture.

When Daniel's thumbs traced the curve of her ears, brailing their contours, the geography of their hills and valleys and hiding places, she became aware that he'd found paradise.

Lifting her face to give those magical hands greater access...she felt one of her earrings hit her shoulder.

Shocked, Ellie opened her eyes. Dear God in Heaven! What was she *doing?*

This was no tropical interlude. The man had her emotions zinging in another way completely.

Daniel, too, looked dazed.

"Are you out of your mind?" she snapped at him, rearing back. "I said you could kiss me. Not—not t-touch me. Look what you've done. You made me l-lose my earring."

Frantically, fighting tears she couldn't explain and angry at herself for being such a sensual pushover, Ellie searched for the silver flower, using her fingers to lightly brush the sand between them, trying not to disturb it overmuch—and trying not to remember another set of fingers that had also lightly brushed, but disturbed very much indeed.

The hibiscus blossom she'd placed in her hair earlier in the evening dropped to the sand, but she swatted it away.

Why was she crying, dammit?

She couldn't find the earring.

Had she only imagined it falling? A subconscious warning, perhaps? Reaching up, she touched the lobes of her ears just to make sure it was truly gone. It was. The other was still there, however.

Taking it out of her ear, Ellie dropped it in the pocket of her skirt so she wouldn't lose it, too, then slowly, carefully stood, trying not to shift any more sand than she must.

As she rose, the lost earring tumbled to the sand.

Snatching it up, she turned to face the man who'd sent her emotions careening out of control.

How dare he presume to…to do what he did! She'd only given him permission for a little nothing kiss between two strangers, a meaningless acknowledgment brought about by a lovely tropical night, not…not something else altogether.

Something that made her want to turn her face into Daniel's broad chest and weep.

How dare he!

But before Ellie could utter a single heated word, her tirade died from lack of direction.

Daniel wasn't there.

Like the irresponsible bum he was, when the going got rough, he simply left.

"Handsome is as handsome does," she muttered darkly, borrowing Gram's favorite saying.

Gathering her sandals, Ellie stomped through the sand to the street and headed for Chad's apartment.

Why didn't I leave when I could? Daniel thought, and groaned silently.

By now the party was dead; only a few "cousins" remained, picking up paper plates and cups, talking and laughing quietly.

Watching them from his usual place among the hibiscus, he would have kicked himself if he could. For whatever reason, freedom was within his grasp and he'd traded it for the company of a pretty girl.

Heck, she wasn't even that pretty.

Beautiful, though, when she smiled. And tonight she'd smiled just for him.

How long had it been since a beautiful woman smiled for his benefit?

But a thousand pretty women could have smiled at him for years to come if he'd just had the presence of mind to leave the damned cove.

He'd known the place for what it was, but just like the first time, he'd let it seduce him again.

Trap him again.

Daniel sucked in a breath he didn't actually have.

Ellie!

She'd run through the shallow water when he was chasing her. But she'd done it in all innocence. Surely the waters of the cove wouldn't punish her for that.

Scanning the garden as far as he could see, Daniel

searched for her, wishing he could somehow literally beat the surrounding bushes.

But though he examined every corner of the yard and beneath every shrub and tree within his field of vision, he saw no trace of a woman with hair the color of moonlight and a smile to rival its glow.

He wouldn't even consider that she might be trapped elsewhere. If the force in the cove was just, it kept its curse only for him.

Yet somehow tonight he'd been released for a while, Daniel thought, a fact offering a glimmer of hope that he would be again.

And if he was...*when* he was...he was outta here.

In the meantime he had something new to think about. What color, he wondered, were Ellie's eyes when the moon didn't wash them to silver?

Chapter Three

On the excuse of checking the coals in the barbecue grill, Ellie let herself out the sliding screen door of her brother's apartment. A gathering of marines and their significant others could be overwhelming.

But here on the patio it was another of the perfect tropical nights Hawaiians considered a norm. An almost full moon rode low in the sky and, upwind, the light breeze carried the scent of flowers she didn't know the name of.

The night was perfect, all right, but it reminded her of Daniel.

Deliberately Ellie stepped downwind to the grill to get a good whiff of burning charcoal, her peaceful mood vanishing at the thought of the man on the beach whose touch turned her to flame.

The cad. Okay, it was an old-fashioned word, but a perfect description of the…bounder.

Perfect. That word again. She was sick of it.

Forty-eight hours ago, on a perfect tropical night on a perfect tropical beach, a man with a perfect face and perfect body had made a perfect fool of her. He'd taken her perfect flirtation and turned it into a…a perfect fiasco.

After three years of careful control, Daniel had blind-sided her, making her heart remember things she didn't want it to remember, making her body feel things she didn't want it to feel.

And the heck of it was, he hadn't even kissed her.

When she'd come back to Chad's apartment after the debacle on the beach, she'd been fiercely glad of that. But it hadn't stopped her traitorous mind from wondering what the man's kiss was like.

Still, if she wanted kisses, there were a couple of single marines in the group behind her who would be glad to oblige, she was sure.

Somehow, though, she doubted it would be the same.

Lifting her face to the moon riding a drifting cloud, Ellie knew she'd been out here long enough. After all, her brother had thrown this shindig so she could meet some of his buddies. It was also a sort of last "oo-rah." Many of them, like her brother, would deploy to Okinawa shortly.

As she turned to reenter the apartment, however, Ellie glimpsed a shadowy figure sitting at a picnic table just beyond the range of light shining through the patio doors behind her.

A tenant from one of the other units, perhaps? But most of them, also marines, were at her brother's party.

Yet there was something about the vague shape…

Ellie walked toward the picnic table. With at least ten good men in the room behind her, she had no reason to be afraid.

Once close enough to get a look at the seated figure, though, her heart lurched. She halted abruptly.

Daniel!

She narrowed her eyes. "What are you doing here?"

From where he sat, the man had certainly been able to see her when she came outside. But he hadn't said a word.

Holy grief, was he *stalking* her?

"There's a whole platoon of marines in there," she informed him tightly, nodding toward the low-level noise behind her when he didn't answer right away. "I suggest you leave while you're still in one piece."

"Love to," he replied, not moving.

"Well, go on." She made a shooing motion with her hand. "If you don't leave, I'll…I'll—"

"You'll call in the artillery," Daniel said, sounding tired. "Go ahead. Maybe that will work." He stood.

In the moonlight Ellie saw his faint, bitter smile. It was the saddest thing she'd ever seen.

But remembering the man's effect on her at the beach, she froze her melting heart right back up again.

Still, when Daniel stretched and rolled his shoulders as if he'd been sitting too long, her gaze couldn't help but follow his rippling muscles.

He wore the same bathing suit he'd had on two nights before, she noticed. Or was it boxers?

A thought that revved her imagination into overdrive.

It was definitely time for this man to hit the road.

"Look," she began with a growl....

"Hey, El. Who you got there?"

Chad had come up behind her and now put out his hand like the friendly Texan he was. "Chad Simms, Ellie's brother," he said.

"Daniel Morgan," Daniel replied.

The two shook hands congenially.

Men, Ellie thought. Did they never stop the good-ol'-boy routine long enough to ask questions?

"Daniel was just leaving," she said.

But she should have known. Her brother had Texas hospitality bred to the bone.

"Why don't you join us?" he invited. "We've got plenty of chow and cold beer, and you'd be welcome."

For a split second Ellie saw a look of such raw longing on Daniel's face that her heart stopped. But the look disappeared when he smiled easily.

"Sorry, but thanks, anyway. I'm, uh, missing my party threads. My clothes were...stolen and..." He shrugged.

"That's been happening on the beaches a lot lately," Chad said. "But hell, buddy, we're about the same size. I'll loan you somethin'. C'mon in."

And that was all it took for Daniel to join their party.

Chad found him a change of clothes, even a pair of shoes. Using the bathroom, Daniel showered, then joined the rest of them, wearing a pair of her brother's khakis and a blue golf shirt, a color that intensified the aquamarine of his eyes.

Several of the other women noticed how well the shirt suited him, too, Ellie saw.

But the man was clearly a survivor. In a room full of

burly marines, he wasn't about to show interest in one of their wives or girlfriends.

Oh, no. He kept his interest for an intent perusal of Chad's CD collection. And no woman there claimed the same attention as the sports page of a week-old edition of the *Honolulu Times* lying on an end table. He even studied the snack platter as if it were a painting by Michelangelo and he an admiring critic.

Daniel's fascination with the mundane was, well, fascinating. And Ellie was fascinated.

Unobtrusively she watched him pick up a potato chip and examine its wavy shape as if the chip were an architectural wonder. Slowly he brought it to his mouth.

His lips opened...the chip entered. And when it touched his tongue, his eyes fluttered shut. He began to chew—carefully, as if each crunch might detonate an explosion.

Ellie watched, mesmerized by the slow, rhythmic movement of Daniel's jaw, the infinitesimal stretch and compression of skin over his cheeks, the tiny arcing purse of his mouth. When at last he swallowed, so did she.

Or tried to. Her throat was dry.

Then her brother handed him a can of beer. "Here you go, Dan. Sorry about your gear getting ripped off. Bummer."

Daniel looked uncomfortable, but lifted the can and nodded toward Chad in a small salute. "Thanks."

When he'd first joined the party and was pressed, Daniel told them his things hadn't been stolen at the beach, as Chad assumed, but at his hotel.

Ellie knew in her bones the man was lying. There were holes in the story big enough to drive a semi through. But her easygoing little brother had no trouble swallowing the tale.

"Don't worry about the threads," he said now. "I'm getting ready to deploy. Weeding out things, you know. You'll be doing me a favor if you keep them. I've got more you can have, too."

"Appreciate it."

Daniel took a swig of beer, and Ellie, feeling like a voyeur, had to turn her head away from the look of absolute pleasure that passed over his features.

Everything the man did became a symphony of the senses, she thought, and felt her face grow warm at the memory of the way he'd touched her on the beach.

When he tasted her potato salad, though, Ellie knew she'd really impressed him.

Chad wanted this party to be an honest-to-goodness, Texas-style barbecue, with beans, potato salad, cole slaw and corn on the cob to go with the steaks, brisket, sausage and chicken he had on the grill.

Everyone who came pitched in, bringing meat, snacks, drinks and side dishes, but Ellie volunteered to make the potato salad, a family recipe and one of her brother's favorites.

The party migrated outdoors when it came time to eat, and she found herself sitting across from Daniel at the picnic table on the side lawn. They weren't the only ones at the long table, but they might as well have been.

Daniel sat with a paper plate full of food in front of him, but instead of diving in as the rest were doing, he stared at it.

"Find a bug?" Ellie asked.

He looked up to give her his quirky grin, the one with the infinite sadness behind it. For a man Daniel had a very expressive face.

"Did you ever notice," he asked, "how perfect the geometry is on an ear of corn?"

"Can't say that I have." She didn't like that word.

"Yeah, guess not." Picking up his fork, he again examined his plate, studying its contents carefully.

From the look on his face, Ellie supposed whatever food Daniel decided to plunge the fork into first would determine world peace.

He chose her potato salad.

Around them the party noise faded to a low murmur. Ellie held her breath.

The fork entered the small hill of potatoes and came up with a good-size sample. In the creamy heap, she saw touches of the pale-green celery she'd added, the darker green of dill pickles, the red of pimento, flecks of brown peeling, golden egg yolk.

When at last Daniel brought the forkful of salad to his mouth, Ellie's lips parted in automatic accompaniment.

He closed his eyes. Chewed. Swallowed.

And his face melted into lines of rapt appreciation.

Ellie exhaled a small satisfied sigh.

"Do you *always* do that?" she asked, after his second bite.

"What?" He forked into the baked beans, but she hadn't made the beans so his reaction to them wasn't of much interest.

"Treat everything as if it were created for your sensual pleasure."

The fork stilled as he gazed back at her. "It's just been a long time," he said at last, with a touch of self-consciousness.

As an answer, the words made no sense at all.

But little about Daniel made any sense, Ellie thought. For one thing, nothing about him seemed to match.

On the beach she'd thought him a handsome footloose beach bum, but tonight he'd been a quiet, unassuming, slightly embarrassed guest, who treated everyone as if they were uniquely special and everything as if it were a gift from the gods.

"A long time since what?"

This time his grin was wide and mischievous, unmarred by any kind of melancholy. "Since I've had such delicious potato salad. You Texans know how to cook."

Ellie grunted. Enough, already.

Leaning forward, she pinned him with her steeliest nurse's look, the one that said, "Don't mess with *me*, buster!"

"So tell me what you're really doing here, Daniel Morgan, and don't crank out any more fairy tales about robberies, either."

But when Daniel lowered his fork without even tasting the beans, she felt as if she'd just told a kid his cookie was full of broccoli bits.

"You wouldn't believe me if I told you," he said quietly.

"Try me."

Daniel eyed the woman across from him and knew by her steady gaze that Ellie wasn't going to let this go.

Yet what could he say that she would believe? Certainly not the truth.

But he gave it to her, anyway.

"The truth is, I can't leave."

And God knew he'd tried.

At first he hadn't known where he was when he found himself again released from Tom and Janie's back garden. He only knew he wasn't back at the cove.

Tonight, though, he appeared to be in someone else's yard, on a lawn surrounding a huge rambling house. Still, the nearby fence looked familiar, and he gazed at it for a long moment in puzzlement, wondering where he'd seen it before.

Then he knew. He'd been looking at it for years, but from the other side.

Hell, he'd gone no further than the house next door!

But he was free! Free!

Remembering what his hesitation cost him last time, he immediately sprinted toward the street that he could see through the trees, as cars passed by with their lights on...and slammed into something that sent him sprawling.

Seeing nothing in his way, he figured he'd tripped, so he gathered himself up and set off again.

This time he took no more than a couple of steps before smashing into something—something he still couldn't see but was solid enough to send him crashing to the ground.

Lying in the grass, he studied the empty yard in front of him, watched a car speed by on the street, its headlights arcing through the overhead branches of the trees.

Next time he took the precaution of keeping his arms outstretched.

One step. Two. Three. Fou— Whap! Something stopped him in his tracks.

No matter how much he sidestepped or backed up, as soon as he started forward an invisible wall appeared, though not always in exactly the same place. It seemed to fluctuate a few feet on some whim of its own, but nevertheless prevented him from getting to the street.

But if the whatever wouldn't let him move in that direction, then he'd leave by the back alley.

A plan that worked like a charm until he neared the Dumpsters. Whap! There it was again.

It took a while and a few ignominious falls for him to finally realize that no matter what direction he took, he could go so far and no farther.

The one direction he refused to try, however, was through Janie and Tom's fence. Better this yard, with its limited freedom, than theirs where he had no freedom at all.

Defeated, he'd finally sat down at the picnic table to look over the house he must belong to now. Country-western music filtered from it out into the night, and through the double patio doors he saw a party of some sort going on.

A barbecue barrel near the patio filled the night air with the smell of charcoal and good times.

As Daniel watched, the door slid open and a woman with hair the color of moonlight stepped out.

Ellie!

She didn't see him sitting there, and he didn't call

out. For one thing, he wasn't sure she *could* see him. Not knowing what the rules were in his new situation—not that he ever had—he didn't take anything for granted.

Then Ellie spotted him, had even been angry with him for some reason, but her brother invited him in and Daniel found himself—for the first time in years—actually under a roof. That was when he realized the *whatever* had now bound him to an apartment house.

Moreover, it actually allowed him to be the normal man he'd once been.

But it wouldn't release him completely.

When the party followed its collective nose to the cooking meat outdoors, Daniel unobtrusively walked toward the street again.

The wall, now several feet farther out, was still there. But it affected only him.

One of the couples at the party had left early, calling good-nights as they walked over the lawn to their car parked on the street. They had no trouble at all passing through the invisible barrier keeping Daniel in.

And now Ellie wanted to know what Daniel was doing here.

Hell if he knew.

But thankfully one of the marines sitting at the picnic table with them asked her a question, giving Daniel a break from the third-degree he knew was coming.

When Chad joined them moments later, the talk became general, full of jokes and references he didn't always catch, but he laughed as heartily as the rest of them.

It was a pleasure just to laugh, and he thought he

faked normalcy pretty well until he saw Ellie eyeing him, a knowing look on her face.

Damn.

As the evening wore on and the party thinned out, Daniel knew he should leave, too. He just didn't know how.

So he hung around, gathering debris in the part of the yard allowed to him, picking up cans and napkins in the living room, trying to look like a conscientious guest helping out a little before going home. By then there were only himself and Ellie and Chad left.

As he tied off a trash bag, Chad clapped him on the back. "Where you sleepin' tonight, Dan?"

Out of the corner of his eye, Daniel saw Ellie's head lift sharply.

"Uh…"

"Bet you don't have a place to crash, do you? Take the couch, man. No problem. I'll get you a pillow and covers."

And before Daniel could protest, Chad had left the room.

He didn't want to stay here, Daniel thought. For one thing, he didn't trust the *whatever* not to also ensnare the innocent people around him. What if he brought some sort of trouble to this brother and sister who'd been nothing but kind to him?

Well, the brother had. Ellie, her pretty face screwed up in a scowl, her silver earrings quivering, looked ready to commit murder.

"You are not staying here," she whispered. "I don't

know what you're up to, but you can find somewhere else to pitch your tent."

"My thoughts exactly," Daniel replied grimly. "Tell Chad I appreciate it, but..."

But Ellie, suddenly feeling small and mean, shook her head a little to silence him.

Whatever Daniel's problem was, she knew for a fact he'd been in the same clothes—or lack thereof—for the last couple of days, at least, and it was obvious to the most hardened soul that he *didn't* have a place to stay tonight.

She sent him a small smile of apology.

"Look, I'm sorry. Of course you can stay if you have nowhere else to go."

Her mother would die if she knew about her oldest daughter's total lack of charity, she thought. After all, this wasn't her apartment. And, really, why was she being so snide?

But Ellie knew. The man rattled her. *More* than rattled her. She blamed him, when it was she who'd overreacted on the beach the other night.

Threading her fingers through her hair, she felt tired to her bones. Even her earrings felt like lead weights in her ears.

Moving to the kitchen counter, she unhooked them and placed them on a paper towel for safekeeping.

"I was being snippy, I guess, because you appeared so suddenly tonight," she said, peering out the darkened window above the sink as she attempted to explain her grudging anger to herself as much as to the man behind her. "And you were rude the other evening."

He didn't answer.

"You could at least have helped me search for my earring before you left that night," she added. "But you disappeared without even saying goodbye."

Still he remained silent.

Slowly Ellie turned away from the dark window to face him.

Daniel was gone.

Again.

Chapter Four

"You lousy beach bum," Ellie screeched at the empty kitchen.

Like magic, Chad appeared from the hallway.

"El?"

"He's gone. Just walked out without so much as a thank-you." Ellie glared at the closed patio door—the only door Daniel could have left by. But how did he leave so quietly?

"He, being...?"

"Who else?" she replied bitterly. "Your good buddy Daniel. Dan. Danny-boy."

"Not my good buddy. I thought he was *your* friend. You were always with him tonight, making sure he got plenty to eat and all. And maybe he was just embarrassed."

Ellie turned her glare on her favorite little brother. Her *only* little brother.

"Not a friend. An acquaintance. I met him, *briefly,* on that little neighborhood beach the other night. He didn't bother with goodbyes then, either. And why should he be embarrassed?"

"Maybe because he had to mooch a bed? And clothes? And food? C'mon, El. Lighten up. You saw the way Dan treated every little thing. He didn't know whether to be greedy or grateful. The poor guy's probably been sleeping on the beach and didn't remember when he'd eaten last before tonight."

"He's a bum, in other words," Ellie said darkly.

Chad gave a stretch and a jaw-splitting yawn. "Nah. Didn't have the look. Just a guy who had everything he owned stolen and is having to do a little unfamiliar begging till he gets things worked out. Happens sometimes. Let's leave the rest of this mess till morning. I'm done and ready to hit the rack."

Translated, he was tired and wanted to go to bed, Ellie thought fondly, giving her brother a quick hug and buss on the cheek before she headed off to her own bedroom.

Sometimes she wondered how Chad managed to survive in the marines. He was far too kind and easy-going. Too accepting.

Anyone else with eyes to see would know that Daniel Morgan was a *bum!* Good-looking, yes. A hunk, yes. Sexy, yes. Uh-huh. But also rude, obnoxious, and...did she say rude?

No goodbye. No thank you. No "I'll call you."

He was a bum.

But all that night Ellie dreamed of the bum, chowing down on a Mt. Everest of her potato salad, bite by slow, sensuous…bite.

Daniel gazed around in disbelief.

Damn! He was back among the hibiscus.

For the first time in years he wanted to kick something, throw himself against his prison, fight his way free of the wood encasing him.

But he didn't.

He couldn't. So he did what was in him to do.

He scowled. Mightily.

A night bird, perched on a nearby branch singing its heart out, strangled mid-note and flew up in alarm, before twittering a snarl at him and flying away in a huff.

Over the next couple of days, Chad showed Ellie more of the island.

Ellie relaxed and enjoyed, content to let her brother do the driving and make the decisions about what they would see. It felt good not to be in charge, for once.

But this close to his deployment date, Chad couldn't spend all his time with her.

Left to her own devices for the day, while her brother did whatever he did on base, Ellie puttered around the apartment, straightening and tidying. There wasn't a lot to do. The marines had apparently cured her brother of the slovenly ways he'd once had at home.

She was carrying a basket of dirty clothes over the lawn and around to the back of the apartment house where the laundry facilities were located when she saw a group of children, Georgie among them, playing baseball in the street.

He waved to her. "Hey, Miss Ellie. Wanna play?"

She did.

And later, with her hair half hanging from its ponytail, her face as sweat-streaked and grimy as her playmates', she tromped with them to Nona's back garden when the old woman called them in for fruit drinks and freshly baked cookies.

"You like children," Nona said, topping off Ellie's glass of passion fruit juice.

Ellie grinned. "Yes. Healthy ones are so much fun." Using an elbow, she dug it gently into Georgie's arm where he'd pressed up against her. He giggled.

"I'd forgotten you were a nurse," Nona replied.

When one of the other children tagged him, Georgie took off in hot pursuit. The women watched the resulting scuffle, both of them smiling.

"I'm glad you've made a friend of that one," Nona said quietly. "Georgie's mother is very sick, so he is staying with us for a while. He misses her."

"Is he your grandchild?"

"My sister's husband's niece's child," the old woman replied with a laugh. "But most of my sister's family live on the Big Island, and Georgie is in first grade here. He stays with us so he won't have to change schools as well as be away from his mother at this time. *Ohana,* you see."

"*Ohana.* I've seen the word somewhere. What does it mean?"

In a blink, the old woman's gaze trapped her own.

Nona touched her hand. "Family," she said. "It means

family. We look after our own no matter how far removed the connection is."

"My grandmother says the same thing, though she doesn't call it *ohana.*" Ellie spoke more for something to say than anything else. The air around her seemed to shimmer.

"Being from Texas, I guess she wouldn't." Nona removed her hand from Ellie's and laughed.

The atmosphere settled into normalcy.

Ellie gave herself a small disgusted shake. What was there about these islands that had her imagining things?

The thought had her glancing toward the corner of the garden dominated by huge hibiscus bushes. Among them, she saw the tiki god—or whatever it was—peeking out. The thing scowled at her.

"Would you like to see my garden ornament again?" Nona asked, following the line of Ellie's gaze.

Without waiting for an answer, the old woman stood and led the way to the tiki's domain.

The two women studied the wooden statue squatting in dignified ugliness under a bush. Plumeria blossoms lay scattered before it. Ellie didn't remember its grimace being so fierce.

Yet something about the eyes, carved deep within the wood, fascinated her. Surrounded as they were by the lines of its stylized scowl, they reminded her of...

"Poor thing," Nona said softly.

"Why?" Ellie, too, whispered.

"Because he's lost and far from home."

Ellie wasn't sure that was the *why* she meant, but she let it go. "You don't think it's Hawaiian?"

Nona pursed her mouth and eyed the carving critically. "No," she said at last, "I don't think so."

Unsure of the figure's significance to the older woman, Ellie had to force herself not to trace her fingers down the side of the ugly face.

"If he's not from here, where could he be from?"

"The mainland, I imagine. He has that look."

"Um, we don't have anything like this on our side of the pond, Nona."

"Of course not, dear." The old woman chuckled. "Where are your plumeria earrings?"

For no reason, Ellie felt she should apologize for not having them on.

"I, uh, don't wear them every day. Only when I'm feeling islandish."

Again, as if at a private joke, Nona chuckled softly. "Islandish. So appropriate."

Not having Ellie's reservations, she reached out and ran a gnarled hand over the tiki's head, much as she would one of the children still playing around them. "Soon, perhaps, you'll go home," she told it placidly, and turned away.

Walking back to the picnic table, Ellie couldn't resist a last glance over her shoulder. The tiki's gaze seemed to follow after them.

But now, through a trick of the light, she supposed, its carved scowl didn't appear quite so fierce anymore.

"Enough touristy stuff," Chad announced when he came in that night. "Get your glad rags on and we'll check out downtown."

"Downtown?"

"Honolulu. We'll eat, maybe do a few clubs."

"Oh, Chad, I don't know. I haven't done the club thing in years. It's not my scene anymore."

"A little music. A little dancing. Won't be more than that," Chad said persuasively. Striking a pose, he did a hip swiveling two-step.

Ellie laughed. "Doofus."

"Hey, you're the one who taught me to dance, big sis. C'mon, it'll be fun."

When she still hesitated, he dropped his bantering. Putting an arm around her shoulders, he led her to the mirror hanging over the sofa.

"Eliza Ann," he said seriously, "how old are you?"

"You sound like Gram when she's getting ready to lecture," Ellie told him with a chuckle.

"Don't change the subject. How old are you?"

"Thirty. There. I've said it. Satisfied?"

He held her gaze in the mirror.

"That's right. Thirty. Not eighty. It's time to play a little, El. You've been working twelve-hour days and call going to the grocery store afterward a night on the town. Now you're calling a medical conference and visiting your brother a vacation."

"Who's been talking?"

"Who do you think? Mom, for one. You never have time to go shopping with her. Dad, for another. Your idea of a Sunday afternoon is watching the Spurs play basketball—on television. And Marlie. Remember the sister you haven't seen in over eight months? She says the only time the babies see their auntie is when she and Caid go to San Antonio."

He gave her a one-armed hug. "You know what our family is like, El. Everyone worries. Gram says you're working yourself into the ground."

Ohana, Ellie thought, and shivered.

At last Chad released her gaze, but only so he could take both her shoulders. "You're young, El. Too young to be sitting at home all the time. And you're pretty. You have a great personality, and you're kind."

"I have all my teeth, too. Chad Simms, are you trying to set me up for a blind date?"

"Would I do that? I'm *trying* to take you dancing before you turn old and senile."

"I'm not that bad, baby brother."

"Yes, you are. Not senile, of course, but cripes, El! Here you are in beautiful Hawaii. Did you put on your bikini and soak up a few rays on the lawn today? Did you hop on TheBus for the cheapest tour going of the island?"

He didn't give her time to answer. "No. You cleaned my already-clean apartment. You washed *clothes,* for cryin' out loud!"

"And I played baseball with the kids next door and visited their grandmother," Ellie replied defensively.

"So tonight you play with the grown-ups. Maybe laugh a little, hmm? You hardly ever laugh anymore, and you used to laugh all the time."

Ellie stiffened. "It's been a rough few years."

"I know," her brother replied gently, and pulled her into a hug. "And I'm not asking you to forget. None of us are. But the family doesn't want you to forget how to be happy, either."

One of the few people who could talk Ellie into anything was Chad. His sweetness did it every time.

"You're sure these old bones can still dance?" she asked with a shaky chuckle, giving in.

"They can if we oil 'em up a little with grilled shrimp and mahimahi. Get a move on."

Without warning, Daniel found himself on the lawn of the apartment house next door. He had just enough time to duck around the corner as Chad and Ellie emerged from it.

If the two found him lurking on the premises again there was no telling what they would think.

But caution didn't keep Daniel from appreciating the short silky skirt and high-heeled strappy sandals that set off Ellie's long shapely legs. And the flow of her silvery hair down her bare back was sheer poetry.

If things were different...

Hell, if things were different, he'd be a married man, probably with a kid or two. He'd have a comfortable, undemanding practice, golf on Wednesdays, and his parents over for dinner on alternate Sundays.

Chad and Ellie got into a car, and Daniel's thoughts ended with a sudden rush of wind he couldn't feel blowing him into...

Nowhere.

Black endless void surrounded him, filled by the wail of the wind, so loud and relentless it beat against his senses till he was totally disoriented.

Sick, nauseated, he wanted to cry out, wanted to cling to something, anything. But he couldn't.

He could only endure.

Willing himself to relax, to reclaim his soul, he sank into the darkness, sank into the roar.

And found himself on a crowded street.

Holy moly! He was in Waikiki! Not only in Waikiki, but walking down Lewers Street—make that half running down Lewers Street. For whatever reason, he had to hurry.

Hurry to do what?

Hurry to catch up with Ellie and Chad, who were ahead of him and also weaving in and out of the crowd.

Still reeling from the maelstrom of moments before, Daniel tried to stop.

His legs wouldn't let him. He had to hurry.

When Chad and Ellie entered a restaurant, however, he could finally slow his pace. Hell, he could *linger…* but only outside the restaurant. Once again, the invisible wall kept him from leaving the area.

It dawned on him, then, that the *whatever* holding him prisoner must have released him, but only into the custody of this brother and sister from Texas.

Make that to the sister. Chad hadn't been with Ellie at the cove that first night, so it seemed to be her presence dictating the length of his chain.

He felt like an organ grinder's monkey.

A monkey left standing *outside* the restaurant, he thought bitterly, while the pretty leash holder was inside, ordering from the seafood menu the place was famous for.

The hell with that. Fishing beneath the waistband of his borrowed trousers and into his money belt, Daniel pulled out a debit card.

* * *

"Chad, it's *him.*"

Her brother, perusing the menu, didn't look up. "Who?"

"Daniel."

"Um. I'm leaning toward the mixed platter. How about you?"

"Stop thinking about your stomach. It's *Daniel!*"

Chad finally looked in the direction of her discreet nod. "Why, so it is. Let's ask him to join us."

And before she could protest, her brother left the table and headed across the room to where Daniel sat perusing his own menu.

Good holy grief.

Would her brother never learn?

In moments Daniel joined them. "Found your money, I see," she commented acidly.

He grinned back at her, a light dancing far back in his eyes, but then looked down at himself still wearing the clothing Chad loaned him a few nights before.

"Good thing I was wearing my money belt," he said. "But my gear is still missing."

So why don't you buy your own? Ellie wanted to ask, but noting the slight stain of red climbing Daniel's neck, she didn't.

Then, as the moment passed, she could have kicked herself. She was as big a pushover as Chad.

Daniel and her brother immediately settled into a deep discussion of the menu, other restaurants and favorite night spots—sounding as if they'd been best buds for years, Ellie thought in disgust.

Giving the two a fake sardonic smile, she excused herself to the ladies' room.

Nothing about Daniel added up, and it was giving her a royal headache.

"Nothing about you adds up," Chad said grimly, as soon as Ellie was out of earshot. His gray eyes, warm and friendly just moments before, now reminded Daniel of a snowy midwinter sky.

"I saw you on the street," Ellie's brother continued. "If you're going to tail someone, you need a few lessons. But take them from an expert because I'm an expert too, bud. You were a fake the other night and you're still one. The White Parrot, the club you recommended for great music, closed two years ago. The tourist you claim to be wouldn't have known it existed. And before you start explaining, here's a piece of advice."

Chad's voice, soft, almost a whisper, held a menace that crawled right up Daniel's backbone.

"If you even think of stalking my sister, I'll have your liver for lunch. And when I'm finished, what's left of the rest of you won't add up to fish bait."

Chad Simms was far more than the friendly, laid-back little brother Ellie assumed he was, Daniel thought. But the man had a right to be suspicious. Hell, he was suspicious himself.

Sitting back in his chair, Daniel allowed the other man's arctic gaze to hold his own.

"I'm not stalking Ellie," he stated quietly. "But I can only give you my word for that because I'm in a…well, a situation that's out of my control."

Chad snorted. "You call that an explanation? Better get more creative. So far I'm not buying it."

"No, I don't call it an explanation. I call it all I've got. Hell, man, I'm still waiting for someone to explain it to me." Daniel faced Chad squarely.

"I can't tell you anything else. Except this. I think you'll be seeing more of me whether I like it or not. Whether *you* like it or not. Bottom line, if you want to beat me to a bloody pulp, you might as well get started."

For a long moment Chad looked back at him, clearly evaluating Daniel's words. "Are you a spook?"

"Maybe. I've thought of it, but what do I know? You could try shooting me. Then we'd both find out."

Surprisingly the other man grinned. "Tempting, but that's not the spook I meant. Are you with the government? Covert ops, maybe?"

Before Daniel could answer, Chad grimaced. "Never mind. Dumb question. If you are, you won't tell me, and if you tell me you aren't, you could be lying."

His voice returned to its soft menacing drawl, and winter returned to his gray eyes. "Listen up, bud. Whoever you are or whatever you are makes me no nevermind because I have a few connections myself. Neither you nor anyone else is involving my sister in something shady or dangerous. Got that?"

"My word on it. I don't know why Ellie seems to be a focus, but I swear to you, I'ddd neverrr huuuurt herrrr....

Chad nearly choked on the drink he'd been about to swallow as Daniel's words drifted into hollowness, sounding as if they came from the bottom of someplace far far away. Even his shape blurred eerily around the edges. Though his body didn't disappear completely, for a couple of seconds Chad could see right through him.

And then Daniel was whole and solid again, but looking disoriented as he lifted a hand to his forehead.

Chad's first thought wasn't spook. It certainly wasn't ghost. It wasn't even denial.

"Gram," he whispered accusingly. "What are you up to now?"

"Sorry," Daniel said, taking a healthy swig from his water glass. "Felt a little woozy there for a second."

You ain't felt nothin' yet, Chad wanted to tell him. "No problem," he said.

At least not mine. But, Dan ol' buddy, you're in for one hell of a ride.

In the ladies' room, Ellie replaced the earring she'd taken out so she could rub her earlobe. She really liked Gram's gift. Their island style gave her a great look when she wore her hair down but tucked behind her ears as she did tonight. But the silver flowers were heavy and after a while became uncomfortable.

Giving herself a last appreciative look in the mirror—so much for old and senile—Ellie pushed through the door to return to their table.

She didn't look half-bad, she was hungry, and she was ready to dance. After all, her persuasive brother only echoed what she herself was thinking the other night at the Kamehanas' luau. It *was* time to play with grown-ups for a while.

Waikiki. What better place to do it?

So what if Daniel seemed to have joined the party? She could handle him.

But could he dance?

Chapter Five

Daniel could dance.

He danced like he did everything else—as if every beat, every nuance in the rhythm in the music found its way to his most basic instincts.

When Ellie danced with him, as she did often, her body caught fire from his, the music binding them in a sensual heat she'd swear turned their two bodies into one. Fast or slow, together or apart depending on what the band played, when Daniel's body moved, Ellie's body followed.

But they never danced together through two sets in a row. Whatever happened on the dance floor was too strong, too powerful to be taken in large doses, the charge between their two bodies threatening a conflagration neither of them wanted.

Yet the joy of the music, the delight of a partner completely in tune with oneself kept them coming back together over and over through the evening.

Ellie had always been a good dancer, but she'd never before taken such pleasure from music. Was it Daniel's influence, or merely the fact she'd decided to emerge from her self-imposed social desert?

At the end of her marriage, she'd sat down and mapped out the path she wanted her life, now her career, to take, deliberately leaving no room in it for remarriage or any kind of significant other. Even so, as Chad pointed out, she didn't have to give up fun.

So tonight she was determined to party, to laugh and dance with anyone who asked her. And she did. With the club a gathering place for Chad's friends, she'd laughed and danced with them all.

She was in Hawaii, for heaven's sake. Aloooo-ha!

Opposite her brother and dancing energetically in the loose style she'd developed tonight after several sets with Daniel, Ellie laughed softly to herself.

"Having a good time?" Chad asked, grinning back at her.

"Yeah. Thanks, little brother, I needed this."

"My pleasure, big sis."

Glancing past Chad, Ellie watched Daniel for a moment as he danced with the same girl he'd danced with two sets earlier and wondered if she herself looked that besotted when she danced with him.

Criminy, she hoped not.

"El, I see a buddy of mine I need to catch before he takes off. Can I take you back to the table for a few minutes?"

"Sure. I'll be fine."

Chad led her to their table, made sure she didn't need anything and hurried across the room to a group of men getting ready to leave the club.

"C'mon, honey. Let's tear up the floor."

Ellie smiled at the attractive man with the engaging grin who stood before her. Though his hair was too long to be one of Chad's marine friends, she'd danced with lots of strangers tonight. So why not?

She soon found out. The music was fast, but the man wanted to hold her tightly in his arms and slow-time it.

"Um, a little too close, Sam. That's your name, right?" Ellie asked politely. Deliberately she distanced their crushed bodies.

Sam pulled her back into a clinch. "Sam, I am," he quipped. "And you're beautiful."

And you're drunk. A shame she hadn't realized that in the first place. "Thanks. Still too close for a first dance, though," she added, and again put a little breathing room between them.

"C'mon, babe, don't be like that."

Sam made another grab at her, but Ellie stopped moving completely as the music stopped. "Oops, no more music," she told him pleasantly. "And here comes my friend."

Daniel approached them, his face like thunder, the woman he'd been dancing with in tow.

"Ellie?"

"This is Sam, Daniel. He's taking me to our table," Ellie explained quickly. Daniel's face didn't wear its usual a-little-sad, a-lot-appreciative look. In fact, his scowl could possibly etch glass.

The woman hanging on to Daniel's hand received most of Ellie's attention, however. She was attractive, if one liked stunning women.

Ellie forgot the importunate Sam completely.

"This guy your boyfriend?" Sam glared at Daniel.

"What? Oh, uh, no."

"Y'all about ready to call it a night?" Chad asked, appearing out of nowhere and pouring on the drawl. "Hate to be a party-pooper, but I have to work tomorrow."

Sam glared at him, too. "Is *this* guy your boyfriend?"

"My brother," Ellie replied absently, her thoughts still on the woman whose hand clung to Daniel's like a stamp on a letter. She gave the woman—oh, and Sam—an empty smile. "Guess we're leaving. Good night."

Finally the woman had sense enough to drop Daniel's hand, though Ellie saw she left a tiny note in his palm. No need to guess what that was.

In no time the three of them were headed down Lewers Street to the car park. "You can hitch a ride back with us," Chad told Daniel offhandedly.

Thinking of his earlier, whirling trip through the black void, Daniel could only be grateful for the invitation. But he sent Chad a sideways glance. The man's attitude had done a complete about-face from what it was earlier in the restaurant.

Though not usually suspicious, Daniel had the uncomfortable feeling that Ellie's brother knew something he didn't. He opened his mouth...and stopped.

Ellie wasn't with them.

Checking over his shoulder, he saw her a couple of stores back gazing into a display window. Even as he watched, Sam and three other men approached her.

He saw her laugh and shake her head, obviously trying to defuse the situation, and then he didn't see her anymore for the massed bodies surrounding her.

Chad got there first, but Daniel was right behind him.

Sam went flying. The others were older and beefier, but not much wiser. One of them pulled a knife while his cohorts brandished beer bottles.

Ellie watched in astonishment as her easygoing, gentle-as-the-proverbial-lamb baby brother became something she didn't recognize.

In seconds one of the men lay still on the sidewalk. But one of his friends attacked Chad from the back while the other scuffled with Daniel.

Daniel, she found, wasn't just a pretty face, either.

When he grabbed a spot at the base of the man's neck, the man howled and dropped to his knees. In seconds he, too, was out of commission. Daniel turned to Chad who had his own opponent's arm pulled high behind his back.

Her brother's face wore a look of such cold purpose that Ellie gasped and turned a little sick inside.

Chad pulled the arm higher. Any more and she knew it would break.

Daniel, it seemed, knew it, too. "I've got a better way," he told her brother mildly. "Hurts a hell of a lot more, but doesn't do as much damage. Watch."

While Chad held the struggling swearing man, Daniel used one long-fingered hand to grasp the would-be attacker's collar bone. His thumb dug in. Hard.

The man screamed, then screamed again as he stared at his useless arm. "You broke it, you son of a—"

"Unh, unh, unh," Daniel said. "There's a lady present. One more word out of you and I *will* break it. Better yet, I'll let my friend here do it. He's not as charitable as I am. Be nice, and you'll get feeling back in that arm in time to stand before a judge."

He glanced toward the street as two policemen emerged from a patrol car. "Why look, here's your cab now."

Later, as Chad unlocked the car, he grinned at Daniel. "You'll have to teach me that one. Where'd you learn something like that?"

Daniel grinned back. "Medical school teaches a whole lot of useful things. But I learned that particular trick as an intern from a doc who'd been around a long time. Gang members in the E.R. don't always know the fight's over once they're on a gurney."

"You're a doctor, huh?" Chad said, as Daniel climbed into the back seat after putting Ellie in the front.

"Yeah."

So he really was an M.D., Ellie thought. Not the beach bum she'd thought at all.

"Why does that not surprise me?" she heard her brother whisper to himself. Catching her eye, Chad grinned at her. She gazed back at him suspiciously.

"Where are you from?" Chad then asked Daniel with an equally suspicious casualness.

"The Hamptons."

A brief answer if ever she'd heard one. The man was just so darn mysterious. Needlessly so.

"Been here long?"

Her brother wasn't much better. After tonight's little display she would never think of Chad in the same way again. Now he was grilling Daniel. Not in an obvious way, but there was something in his voice….

"A few years, I think," Daniel replied quietly.

You *think?* Ellie turned to look at Daniel over her shoulder, but in the intermittent glare of passing streetlights, he looked so troubled she didn't have the heart to pursue it.

Apparently Chad didn't, either, because he allowed the conversation to drop. In the quiet car, Ellie scrooched down in her seat and put her head against the backrest. Reaching up, she removed her earrings.

Later, she thought. *I'll ask him about it later.*

But later didn't come. By the time the car stopped and Ellie woke up enough to pull herself together, Daniel was gone.

Daniel drowsed among the hibiscus, thinking of the evening before—the almost sensory overload of good food, good music and being in a milling crowd, being touched, bumped into and jostled by sweaty, pulsating bodies. He'd enjoyed it all.

But most of all he thought of Ellie, her usual suspicion forgotten as she danced with him, her movements matching his so perfectly that he thought of soul mates and miracles.

Okay. So perhaps the soul mates part was a little extreme.

But wasn't it all a miracle? One of the things he'd learned in the Kamehanas' garden was that people forgot how truly wonderful being alive was. Once upon a time, he hadn't known it, either, taking what he had for granted.

And he had a lot—money, position, an old family name. Yet, now those things were distant memories and not very important ones at that. He'd learned from the Kamehanas what emotional poverty he'd actually lived in.

But last night? Worth a small fortune.

The light tickle of a plumeria lei being placed around his neck brought Daniel out of his reverie.

Here was another miracle in his confined life. Something he could do. It wasn't much, and he wished with all his heart he could do more, yet in this one small way he could make a difference in a world that no longer let him in.

When Nona placed a lei of plumeria around his neck, he could "talk" to her, though he wasn't sure how. Certainly not with his voice. He didn't have one here. Yet she understood him.

But only when he wore the plumeria lei.

Nona was worried. One of the children had run a low-grade fever during the night and this morning was dragging around and cranky, as Nona put it. Was it the flu, rampant throughout the islands lately, or merely a bad cold?

Tell me the symptoms.

As the old woman talked about the child—Mary Ann, this time—Daniel listened carefully. He concluded it was merely a cold, but without examining the little girl he couldn't be positive.

Nona, however, thought it was a cold, too. She patted his cheek, though Daniel didn't actually feel it, and went away.

If he could, Daniel would have smiled. Nona was

quite the diagnostician in her own right. Mainly she came to him just to have her opinion confirmed, though on occasion he'd picked up on things the old woman hadn't.

He'd once been a good doctor, Daniel thought, excelling in diagnosis both in medical school and on the floor as a resident. His analytical turn of mind, he supposed, combined with a less explainable intuition.

"A gift," one of his superiors labeled it. As Daniel recalled, the doctor had been angry.

Looking back, he now knew why. While he could usually figure out what was wrong, the patient was never more to him than a problem to be solved.

It was a joke among his fellow interns that Daniel couldn't remember names. Room 210 was "the spleen." Room 640 "the appendectomy."

Not faces—cases. As a doctor he'd been good; as a person he'd been a horse's behind.

Which brought his thoughts back to Ellie. A pediatric nurse, she'd said. He'd bet she knew each of her small patient's names. With her heart-stopping smile, she'd have them in the palm of her capable hand. Look how she charmed Georgie the other night.

And him, Daniel thought. Wasn't he totally charmed by the woman, too? Well, not completely. It was hard to be completely charmed by the person who held the keys to his freedom.

But still, watching Ellie let herself go on the dance floor last night was something he would remember the rest of his life.

Or until he rotted away.

* * *

Chad was up and gone for the day by the time Ellie awoke the next morning. She didn't remember the last time she'd slept in like this.

Beyond making her bed and cleaning up her breakfast dishes, she ignored the light clutter in the apartment and went to the bus stop a half block away.

Nona was there. "Aloha," the old woman greeted her. "Where are you going this beautiful morning?"

Ellie laughed. "I don't know. Chad said if I got on TheBus it would take me all around the island. So I'm off on an adventure to unknown places."

"Adventure," Nona repeated as the two of them took adjoining seats. "So where are you going when you leave Hawaii?"

Startled, Ellie looked at her. "Why, I'll go back to Texas. I have a job in San Antonio, you know."

"I know. Do what you do best, my dear, but don't forget to add adventure. You were made for it."

"You sound like my gram," Ellie said with a laugh. "She talks like that, too. Are you predicting my future?"

"Only reminding you of its wonderful possibilities," Nona replied placidly. "The choice is always yours. Ah. Here's the pharmacy. Mary Ann has a cold."

As the old woman rose from her seat, Ellie asked her impulsively, "What *do* I do best, Nona?"

"Your gift is loving and caring, dearling. But you have to allow yourself to receive it, before you can truly give it to another."

She patted Ellie's cheek as if Ellie were one of her many grandchildren. "Enjoy your day."

And Ellie did. School kids and senior citizens, workers and tourists like herself, she talked with them all as TheBus careened down Kamehameha Highway through some of the worst traffic she'd ever seen.

Past Kualoa Beach and Laie Point, around the North Shore, and a stop off at the Dole Plantation, Ellie experienced the daily bustle of Oahu.

A shame Daniel wasn't with her. With his capacity for sensory enjoyment, he would have loved it.

Now where did that thought come from?

Deliberately, Ellie asked the Asian woman beside her a question about the passing scenery.

By the time she got in that afternoon, she was tired but exhilarated, and already planning what she would do the next day.

When Chad arrived home, he found her in the kitchen adding spaghetti to boiling water.

"You don't have to do that, El. We can go out, or order in. No work for you on this vacation, remember?"

"This isn't work. I never cook at home except in the microwave. Or do you mean you're not interested in Mom's spaghetti sauce? This is her recipe."

"In that case, keep slaving over that hot stove, sis. Give me a minute to change and I'll make the salad."

Ellie had the ingredients out and ready for him when he came back.

"So," her brother said casually, tearing into a head of lettuce, "what did Gram give you?"

Both of them knew what he was really asking.

"Earrings. But I made sure she bought them before I accepted them."

"Ah. Those flower things you wore last night?"

"Plumerias. 'The flower of Hawaii,' the box says. A *department store* box," Ellie emphasized. "Gram wanted to give me a lei made of seashells but I wouldn't take it."

"Smart girl. Let me see 'em."

"What? My earrings? She *bought* them, I tell you. I asked her."

"No big deal, El. I just want to see them up close."

Ellie went to the bedroom and returned with the earrings, now in their original box where she kept them.

"Pretty," Chad said, examining one closely. "Just like a real flower dipped in silver."

"The box says they're sterling." Ellie, too, admired the gleaming blossom in Chad's large hand. It looked dainty and slightly exotic.

Gram had good taste.

"They look nice on you," Chad said. "Put them on."

Ellie's brows shot up. "Why? I'm wearing earrings already and these hurt my ears after a while. You saw them on me last night."

"Just wear them during dinner," Chad told her persuasively. "They'll dress up the occasion since we're not going out."

Dress up the occasion?

But after a moment, Ellie shrugged. Anything for her favorite brother.

Removing the plain gold studs she usually wore, she inserted her grandmother's gift in her earlobes, liking the way she felt when she wore them. They had a way of reminding her she was a woman.

Turning to Chad, she made a show of displaying each ear.

"Nice. Finish up the salad, will you? I'll take the trash out."

Surprised, Ellie watched him tie off the half-full trash bag. He might be a big bad marine, but Chad had the attention span of a gnat.

When he returned to the kitchen from the outdoors, her brother wasn't alone.

"Look who I found," he said.

Chapter Six

Ellie tried to be snippy. She really did.

But it didn't last long. For one thing, her brother's bantering had a way of overriding her own caustic comments, and for another...well, she just didn't *want* to be suspicious and defensive.

This was Hawaii. Land of beaches and the easy good times not a part of her life in Texas, but under Chad's prodding, she could enjoy here.

A-loooow-ha!

To her surprise, she also found she didn't like it when something she said made Daniel suddenly look sad or self-conscious. She didn't even comment on the fact that he still wore the khakis and blue golf shirt Chad loaned him almost a week ago, though he looked as clean and freshly shaved as he was the night they went dancing.

The man had secrets. Let him keep them.

Her brother, however, rustled him up a fresh pair of shorts and a T-shirt. The island uniform, Ellie decided.

With Daniel's ash-brown hair and deep tan, the clothes suited him. He had great legs, too—long, muscled, with a light dusting of golden hair that emphasized their tan. The loose shirt showed off the breadth of his chest and the natural width of his shoulders.

He carried himself with an easy grace, too, Ellie noticed, the kind of understated grace that came from years of knowing exactly who he was.

In a nutshell, Daniel looked like a Ralph Lauren model, she thought, watching him dish up spaghetti from the pot on the stove. The Hamptons, he'd said. Apparently he wasn't lying about that, either.

Glancing across the table, Ellie saw Chad's smirk as he watched her watch Daniel.

She kicked him.

"Hey! That hurt," her brother said, deliberately raising his voice.

Daniel turned from the stove. "Something wrong?"

"Just my brother, being obnoxious," Ellie answered. She'd have a *meaningful conversation* with Chad later.

"Do you have brothers and sisters, Daniel?" she asked, digging into her own spaghetti.

"I'm an only. How about you two? Any more at home?"

"Our sister, Marlie," Chad replied. "Married, with twin babies. They keep her out of trouble, usually."

"Usually, huh?"

"Yeah. You might say our family runs to trouble. Our gram—"

"We also have plenty of aunts and uncles and cousins," Ellie broke in. Gram was no secret, but people who didn't know her could get the wrong impression.

"I have a few of those, too, but not many. My family doesn't get together often. At funerals now and again. That sort of thing."

"Bummer. You should see Gram's backyard on Sunday afternoons. Cousins so thick you have to wade through 'em with hip boots," Chad said with a laugh, but Ellie heard the homesickness in his voice.

"This spaghetti is really good," Daniel told her, well into his third helping.

"Thanks." Ellie loved to cook, but not for herself. It was a pleasure, though, to cook for someone who liked to eat.

But Daniel was still on the subject of family. "*Ohana,*" he said. "The Kamehanas have cousins over on Sundays, too."

"*Cousin* cousins, or cousins?"

"Both."

Ohana, Ellie thought, and sighed. She loved Grammie's Sunday afternoons, though she hadn't been to one of the weekly gatherings for months.

Longer than that. Since her divorce. Since…

"Do you know the Kamehanas well?" Chad asked Daniel.

Another one of those seemingly innocent questions that made Daniel put on his guarded look.

"Well enough to be there on Sunday afternoons," he replied, "but I'm not a relative, no."

"I saw Nona this morning," Ellie commented. "She said one of the children had a cold."

"Yeah, she thought it might be the flu, but we decided probably not."

"You're their doctor?"

"Uh, no." Daniel looked uncomfortable again. "Nona just...asks my opinion on occasion. When she needs actual treatment, she goes to her own physician. A real one."

There was a trace of bitterness in that last, but Ellie held her tongue. What did he mean, a real one? Had Daniel perhaps lost his license?

The talk turned general after that, and neither she nor Chad asked their guest any more personal questions.

Nor did Daniel volunteer any personal information. He talked freely about the Kamehanas, however, but in the kindest possible way, his affection for them obvious. And he talked about the islands and his delight in the various cultures that called them home.

As the three cleaned the kitchen, they talked a little of everything and of nothing much at all.

"Why don't we sit outside for a while," Chad suggested, hanging up his dishtowel. "It's too nice a night to stay indoors."

So they talked and joked around some more while sitting at the picnic table on the side lawn. But when the phone rang, Ellie's brother excused himself to take the call inside.

What had been easy conversation left with him.

"Beautiful evening," Ellie commented at last.

"Yeah, it is."

Silence.

"A few clouds on the horizon, though. Do you think it will rain tomorrow?"

"Might. It's the right time of year for it."

But Ellie had been wondering about something and biting her tongue for the last couple of hours.

"Daniel," she asked suddenly, "did you lose your license?" She didn't understand why it was so important that she know this, but it was.

He looked blank. "My driver's license? No, I still have it." At least he supposed he did, assuming his mother had his effects. His license was in the wallet he'd left in his pants pocket on the beach.

"Your license to practice medicine is what I meant," Ellie said. She didn't look at him but at the treetops rising above the Kamehanas' back garden.

Daniel reared back. "*No* I didn't lose my license! Whatever gave you that idea?"

"You're, ah, cagey sometimes," Ellie said, "especially about being a doctor. It's like something you don't want to talk about. I'm sorry if I offended you."

"I earned my degree in the usual way," Daniel said tightly. "Long hours and little sleep. I assure you my license—general practice, by the way, nothing fancy—didn't come out of a cereal box."

"I said I was sorry." Ellie's voice was small.

"Yes, well..." He sighed. "Look, I'm sorry I sound secretive. It's just that since I've been in Hawaii, I've had...well, I've had some, uh, weird experiences. You see, I took this trip...this tour, and I...well, I...there's things...strange things...that are damned hard to, um, talk about, you know?"

He hoped Ellie knew because he sure as hell didn't.

What he did know was that to anyone rational, or to

anyone from the mainland, he wasn't making a great deal of sense. Ellie, bless her, was staring at him with her sweet mouth agape.

All right. He deserved it.

Ellie straightened. She'd heard those same words and that same tone of voice from dozens of cousins over the years. Not Daniel's *exact* words, of course, but halting phrases containing the same bafflement at a skewed universe. Her cousins wore the same look Daniel had on his face now, too.

She remembered a garbled phone call full of half sentences about blue feathers from her sister, Marlie, a couple of years ago.

Not that Marlie wasn't happy *now,* mind you.

Leaving her place across the picnic table from Daniel, Ellie came around to sit beside him. Acting on pure instinct, she took his hand but kept the presence of mind not to look at him.

There be temptation.

Instead, the two of them sat quietly, their backs now to the table, their faces toward a shadowy horizon.

"Let me tell you about my grammie," she said at last.

Daniel smiled down at this woman made of moonlight, treasuring the warmth of the small hand that filled his in just the way a woman's hand ought to fill a man's.

Odd that nothing in his life had ever felt so right.

She didn't seem to appreciate the moment, however, because she didn't smile back at him—a small fact bringing Daniel back to his own reality with a vengeance.

Here he was, feeling warm and fuzzy over a woman who held the key to his prison. He kept forgetting that.

Letting go of Ellie's hand, he put his elbows on the tabletop behind them so he could slouch, legs extended, ankles crossed.

He hoped the casual look was convincing because what he really wanted to do was wrap his arms around this woman and never let go.

"What about your grammie?" he asked stiffly.

"Well, she... What's that?"

Music floated out to them, soft as a whisper, delicate as fine lace, yet strong enough to fill the night with enchantment. Voices sang and became ocean breezes and star maps; drums beat the echo of ancient hearts, and the notes of a flute, almost below the ear's hearing, carried a promise of eternal tomorrows.

Daniel took Ellie's hand. He had this moment, he thought, and there wasn't room enough in it for holding back.

"It's Nona," he said softly. "She meets with a group some nights and sings."

When Ellie didn't answer, he leaned forward to see her face and found it awash with silent tears.

His heart dropped to his knees. It wasn't the beauty of the music that moved her, he knew, but its truth. Hadn't he, too, once silently wept when Nona sang? And been cleansed?

Acting on pure instinct, he pulled Ellie into his arms. And she, as naturally as she'd placed her hand in his a moment ago, turned her face into his chest and sobbed.

"Can you tell me?" he whispered when her sobs

gradually weakened into small hiccups and ended completely on a long exhausted sigh.

She didn't lift her head, but lay with her weight against him. Nona's music softly swirled, so much a part of the night that the night would have been incomplete without it.

"I lost my baby to SIDS," Ellie said.

Daniel pulled her even closer, hunching his body protectively around hers, as if to shield her against such horror.

No shield existed for something like this.

"I'm a pediatric nurse," she said tiredly, probably repeating what she'd told herself a million times. "I knew all the precautions to take. I was always careful. Always. And yet…"

"Yet it happened," he finished for her, when her words trailed off.

"Her name was LeAnne."

"Tell me about her."

Nona's music whispered through the breeze.

"She was perfect," Ellie said, and rubbed her cheek against his chest right above his heart. "And as sweet as they come."

He heard the mother's smile in her voice.

"Always happy and kicking, eager to see new things. Big gray eyes like Chad's and Marlie's. Fat little baby feet."

She sighed. "I can't think why I'm telling you this. I don't talk about her usually. It's been three years but it still hurts."

"I imagine it always will," Daniel replied quietly.

"But if talking about her keeps LeAnne close to you, isn't that a good thing?"

Her answering chuckle whuffled through his shirt.

"Thank you, Dr. Phil," she said. "What makes you so wise tonight?"

"Doctor who?"

"Phil. Don't tell me you don't know who Dr. Phil is."

"Ah," Daniel said wisely.

Ellie laughed again. Then sighed. "Yes," she said. "Talking about LeAnne is a good thing. And I think I just found that out."

In Nona's music, ocean breezes blew away sadness, and star maps guided the way. Hearts beat through countless generations with a promise of tomorrow just over the horizon.

Ellie told Daniel about a small miracle named Le-Anne that was hers for a while. And then she was silent.

Daniel threaded his fingers through Ellie's silky silvery hair, and a thumb brushed lightly against one of her flower earrings.

She lifted her head.

There wasn't a power in the universe strong enough to keep him from kissing her. He'd been wanting to do it, *needing* to do it, since that first night on the beach.

Nor was he surprised when her lips, warm and full and giving, joined his and melded. After all, the music of the night promised this moment, and this moment was all he had.

His lips to hers, tongues meeting, mating. His heart slamming against her breast.

Breaths stopped, gasped, joined.

And Ellie, slowly but relentlessly, pulled her lips from his.

Nona's music came to an end.

Ellie's forehead needed his to support it for a moment.

"Aloha," Daniel whispered.

"That was not a good thing," she replied, her voice a quavery whisper.

Was that sadness he heard, or determination?

"I thought it a very good thing."

"No." A pause. "After LeAnne died, I dedicated my life and my nursing to children. It was my promise to her. Being a nurse is not only what I do, it's what I am. And what I'll always be."

It was a farewell speech, Daniel knew. Every cell of his body felt every cell of hers rejecting him, though she didn't move.

"Tell me about your grammie," he said quickly, to keep her here.

A flute trilled from the Kamehanas' back garden. Then, silence.

Ellie pulled away from his embrace, but thankfully not his side. No part of her body touched his, however.

Again the two of them sat with their backs to the picnic table, their faces toward the night. Together, but apart.

Better than nothing, he supposed.

But not much.

How the heck had that happened?

Ellie wanted to pinch herself, just to see if she were dreaming. Her innards may have melted to blissful mush, but something wasn't right here.

She'd just cried all over Daniel Morgan's shirt—Chad's shirt. She, who hadn't wept for LeAnne since the funeral.

And she'd told Daniel about LeAnne, not just about her death but about her sweet baby ways. She, who hadn't been able to think about the sweetness of LeAnne even when she went to the grave side, had actually chuckled over the wonder of her baby's chubby little feet.

And somehow, in some strange way, it was finally all right to talk about those wonderful things.

Where Daniel's caress had scared her witless on the beach the other night, tonight it somehow liberated her. She felt lighter.

"A burden shared is a burden halved," Gram always said.

She hadn't been able to share her grief with Kenneth, Ellie thought, and Kenneth hadn't been able to share his with her. No surprise there. They'd rarely been able to share anything. Only LeAnne had held them together, and at her death they'd parted ways.

Nor was she able to discuss it with her family, no matter how tactful they tried to be. Yet tonight she'd cried in the arms of a complete stranger.

All right. After the last few meetings, Daniel wasn't a *complete* stranger, but he wasn't family, either.

And that kiss! Admittedly, she'd been waiting for him to kiss her since the night at the beach. As one of the most sensual men she'd ever met, she'd wondered what Daniel's kiss would be like, even fantasized about it.

Tonight she learned it was all that fantasy and more. Much more.

No more.

Whatever was going on here, it wasn't going any further. She had her life planned, thank you very much, and it didn't include danger with a capital Daniel.

When she left Hawaii, this man and his kisses were staying behind.

But, oh, the temptation of the moment! She was here and he was here. Surely, if she was very careful…

Heck, if she was very careful, she would leave this beach-blanket doctor in the sand where she'd found him.

As it was, Daniel sat quietly beside her, making no further attempt to touch her.

He was aware of her, though. His awareness literally pulsed through the air around them, now that the music had stopped. But she could handle Daniel.

They could…talk. Wasn't that what she'd set out to do in the first place?

Gram. He wanted to know about Grammie.

"Have you ever heard of the Iq'nata tribe?" Ellie asked casually.

"Icknatah? Can't say I have. South American? African?"

"Hybrid North American. Pronounced Ick-na-ta."

"And are they?"

"Are they what?"

"Icky."

"My sister, Marlie the punster, would love you," Ellie told him, but inched a teeny bit closer.

Marlie had her own man. This one was taken.

For the moment.

"So tell me about the Iq'nata tribe," Daniel said. "Are you a member?"

"Yes and no. My grandmother is a great-granddaughter several times removed from the original shaman, so all of us have that connection. And though we're all guessing Gram herself is a member, none of us is positive. Like most tribes, you have to be born into it, but with the Iq'nata, you also have to be accepted into it. The thing is, once you are, not even your family will know for sure. That's how the tribe stays undetected by historians and anthropologists."

"Interesting. What makes you think your grandmother is a member?"

Ellie shot him a sideways look. The man had just digested that piece of ambiguous information without so much as a hiccup. How much more could he swallow?

"Because of her gifts," she replied.

"She has particular talents?"

"A talent for merging physics and philosophy and a talent for trouble, but other than that, I don't think so. Maybe. With Gram, you never know."

She sighed. This was always so hard to explain.

"But I don't mean that kind of gift. I mean the regular kind that comes wrapped in pretty paper for a birthday, or when one of us goes on a trip. *Especially* when one of us goes on a trip or a vacation."

"What's so special about her presents?"

Ellie cleared her throat. "When she gives you something of her own, odd things happen."

"Such as?"

The man wasn't appreciating the nuances of her story, Ellie could tell. Not many did.

"Take my cousin Noelle," she said slowly. "Several years ago she went away to tennis camp. She runs one every summer. It so happened she needed an extra trunk, so Gram gave her an old one she had. The key to it was on a ring with other keys, and since neither of them could get it off, Gram told Noelle to just take the whole bunch."

She shot Daniel a sideways look. "This sounds a little silly when I tell it."

"Hey, don't stop now."

She heard the smile in his voice, though a cloud chose that moment to pass in front of the moon and she couldn't see his features. When had his arm gone around her again?

"She came home with a 1976 VW bus and her first boyfriend."

"And your family was horrified," Daniel concluded. "Can't say I blame them, but how do the keys and the trunk fit in?"

"The trunk doesn't, but the keys do. One of them was the key to that very bus. And the family was delighted. You see, Noelle was thirty-two, had almost no self-esteem, and she brought home a twenty-one-year-old hunk absolutely besotted with her. They've been married seven years now, are as much in love as ever, and have five kids with another on the way."

"And that's bad?" Daniel asked, sounding confused.

"I didn't say it was *bad*. I said it was *odd*. Noelle was smart, attractive, maybe a little sports obsessed, but she deserved to be happy. That's not what was odd. It was the *bus* that was odd. It belonged to the boyfriend."

"Ah."

The moon came out, and Ellie snuggled deeper under his shoulder. Tropical nights could be chilly.

"You see, it was the exact same bus Noelle's parents, my aunt and uncle, had when they were young. They were a little wild back then, Gram said. A couple of their children were conceived in it, we found out. Not that we really wanted to know that."

When Daniel chuckled, she laughed, too.

"Anyway, my aunt and uncle were in a rut and definitely not wild anymore. The story goes they were bored with their jobs and each other, and probably headed for matching midlife crises. But when that bus came back into their lives it breathed new life into their relationship. They retired and now tool around the country saving trees."

"Wow," Daniel said, and laughed again. "You're right. That's odd. And things like that happen when your grandmother gives you something?"

"A personal gift," Ellie emphasized.

"But no one gets hurt?"

"No. At least, not in the end. Sometimes there's a lot of hurt to get to that point, though. It's all in how you choose, Gram says. Everything is a choice and we can take it or leave it. The Great Ones don't care."

"The Great Ones?"

"Another Iq'nata mystery. None of us is clear whether they're gods or spirits or actual members of the Iq'nata tribe, but they're the ones who put choice in our path, according to Gram. We're all born into the tribe, whether we're members of it are not. We're all family,

I guess you could say, and The Great Ones look after family."

Criminy, Ellie thought. She sounded like Nona.

"Let me get this straight. Your grammie's little gifts somehow bring choice into your life, whether you want it or not. You can choose as you will, thereby taking a chance for great happiness. And you don't think this is a good thing?"

"Daniel," Ellie said slowly, "I listened to you earlier this evening when you talked about strange things happening to you, and I heard your voice as you said it. That's why I decided to tell you about Gram. To show you that I understood.

"'I can't explain,' you said. 'There are things here you don't want to mess with.' You sure didn't sound like that was a good thing. How do *you* like having events slip away under your feet?"

"Oh, God, Ellie. It's horrible. Horrible!"

And Daniel sounded so wretched that Ellie turned into his arms and held him tightly within her own.

He sighed. "There's a difference between my story and yours," he said. "Even though I went on vacation before opening my own practice, I didn't have a grammie to give me a parting gift. The East Coast Morgans just don't *do* the Great Ones, you see. Or have grammies. Grandmère Morgan wouldn't take kindly to the name." His voice was bitter.

"I never had a choice. Or maybe I did. Of course I did. I chose to trample all over others' beliefs. And now I'm stuck with it."

Reaching up, Ellie touched his face lightly, wishing

she had Marlie's gift of saying the right thing, or Chad's gift for getting to the heart of a problem.

She had neither, but she could feel Daniel's pain as well as she could feel her own at how lost he sounded.

"Gram says no one is ever stuck with anything," she said.

Daniel turned his face so that his lips found their home in her palm. "Your gram never went swimming in the cove."

"Is that what you did?" Ellie whispered, mesmerized by Daniel's breath trickling through her fingers.

He kissed her knuckles before gently giving the hand back to her.

"And more, I'm sorry to say," he told her sadly. "God knows I've learned my lesson, but now you—"

"Am I intruding?" Chad asked.

Chapter Seven

Ellie jumped. "No! I mean..." She strove for a reasonable tone. "No, Daniel and I were just talking."

She moved slightly, but Daniel didn't take the hint and remove his arm from around her shoulder. Instead, he gazed steadily back at her brother.

Good holy grief! Just what she needed—a display of macho possessiveness on the one hand and brotherly protectiveness on the other.

Ready to set these two roosters straight, she'd just opened her mouth when Chad settled it.

"Well, then. Good night," he said.

Her brother's voice held no aggression that Ellie could hear, but Daniel removed his arm from her shoulder and slowly sat up straight.

"I'd like to oblige, man," he said evenly, "but like I

told you the other night, sometimes I'm forced to hang around for a while."

Ellie gaped at him. What in the world was he talking about?

Chad seemed to know. Her brother laughed. "Nah. You guys talk all you like. Myself, I'm a workin' man and I've gotta get up in the morning. G'night."

Kissing Ellie lightly on the cheek, Chad strode back into the apartment—looking, she thought, like he used to when he grabbed the last drumstick off the platter.

She gave Daniel a narrow-eyed look. "What do you mean you're *forced* to hang around? What did you tell Chad the other night?"

"I told him I have no choice but to be here sometimes," Daniel said quietly. "And he seemed to understand. A good thing too, because God knows I don't."

"Don't what?"

"Understand. There's something about you, Ellie, that…that—"

"This isn't about me," Ellie broke in, her voice as cold as she could make it through the knot of betrayal she felt.

Forced to hang around! And she'd thought he was hanging around simply because he liked her. The jerk.

Daniel drew in a breath. To explain, she assumed.

She glared at him. "Before you say a word, buster, listen up. I don't want to hear any manure about how attracted to me you are. Attraction is a want-to kind of thing, not a, quote, forced-to kind of thing."

Turning her face away from him, she managed to keep her voice coldly even. "Leave out the mush and tell me what Chad knows that I don't. I want in on this big secret, so spit it out."

"I'm trying to," Daniel replied mildly.

Ellie's head whipped around so she could shoot him a look from the far length of the picnic table.

"And you *are* the attraction," he added.

The man just would not take her seriously. "That's it. Do your talking to the local badge because I'm calling the law if you're not gone in thirty seconds."

Daniel remained where he was, and when he spoke, it was with the tired voice he used sometimes, that tone that seemed to carry a burden he didn't know how to share.

"Will you give me a little more time if I start at the beginning?" he asked quietly.

But Ellie was through being a pushover.

"That's exactly where you'll start, but only if my name isn't in it."

"If I'd known you in the beginning, maybe none of it would have happened," he said. "But I was a different person then, so probably it would have. For one thing, I *was* a person, and now I don't know what the hell I am."

Ellie, who had slowly sat back down on the bench, stood again.

"This isn't easy," he said.

"So what is? The beginning or nothing. Facts. No side-bar editorials. Don't give me philosophy."

She actually felt him draw in a breath, hold it a second, then slowly let it out again.

"Okay, just the facts," he muttered.

In the moonlight, she saw the strain in his face.

"I can do that," he said softly, as if to himself. "I think I can do that." He rolled his shoulders.

"Right. Fact. Four years ago—time's kind of gotten lost, but it was four years, I think—I completed my residency and had a brand-new medical degree with the ink on it not even dry. Even so, I was set to step into a thriving practice."

He paused. "The world, as they say, was my oyster. I was engaged to a girl I'd known all my life…"

Ellie's heart dropped.

"…and both her parents and mine were busily planning our wedding. A friend of my father's offered me a partnership in his private clinic with the understanding I would buy him out when he retired in a few years. I would start there after my honeymoon."

Glancing at Ellie, Daniel smiled. "Family practice. I had no interest in specializing."

"Sounds like a neat package," Ellie managed.

"Oh, it was. Almost too neat. Even then I thought so. And maybe that's why, before I found myself nicely tied up in a bow, I decided to come to Hawaii for a few weeks."

"Four years is a long few weeks. What about the girl you were engaged to?"

"She joined me a few days after I got here. We'd vacationed together before, but this time all we did was fight. The irony was that we fought over things I'd thought settled long ago. How many kids we wanted, which town we'd live in, what kind of house we'd buy. Everything."

He shook his head. "You can imagine what it dwindled down to."

"'If you love me, you'll do it my way,'" Ellie replied. She knew those tactics well.

"Yeah. That's when I realized I *couldn't* do things her way. When she accused me of not loving her, I did the gentlemanly thing and denied it, of course. But it was an iffy thing on both our parts, and we both knew it. A pity, because we'd kind of hoped we could be in love, you know?"

"No, I don't know. If you weren't sure you loved each other, why were you getting married?"

Daniel's chuckle held little humor.

"I'm a Morgan, Ellie. Banks, stocks, a railroad or two—generations of old and comfortable money. Laura's parents are Neubauers, ditto the banks, stocks, et cetera. Love and marriage were not synonymous for either of us. Her parents wanted it, my parents expected it, and I'd already stretched their patience to the limit by insisting on medical school."

Again he laughed. "My little hobby, my parents liked to think of it. To their minds, college was something well-bred young men simply did. A good place for me to make useful contacts before joining my father in handling my inheritance."

"Oh."

"Yeah. Anyway, Laura flew back to the mainland to make final wedding plans and I stayed on here to finish my fling. But I was still angry."

Daniel stood and again rolled his shoulders.

"I threw myself into the Waikiki party scene like you wouldn't believe," he continued, taking a stance with one foot on the ground and the other on the bench. "But the harder I tried to have a good time the madder I got, and I didn't know why. That's when I found myself on a 'Spirit of Hawaii' night tour."

Ellie couldn't imagine the man before her doing such a thing. He must have been really bored.

"The kind that takes you to haunted buildings and fills you full of ghost stories?"

"Not quite. This one took us to various ancient sites around the island. The guide gave each of us a small bundle of salt, told us to stay off the grounds themselves, and warned us to speak respectfully of what we saw."

"But you didn't."

"My bundle of salt found a trash can before I even got on the bus."

He sat down again. "Everywhere we went on that tour I proved just how big a fool I could be," he added in self-disgust.

"Some of the sites seemed little more to me than a pile of rocks, and I said so. I even picked up stones at a couple of places and threw them further onto the pile, daring whatever was there to come and get me. By the time we arrived at the cove, the guide and most of the others were justifiably disgusted with me. When I decided to stay there, not one of them tried to talk me out of it."

"The cove you're talking about is the one near here?"

"That's the one. It's a sacred site to the ancient ones, the guide said. And while the ancients are willing to share its beauty, they won't share its waters. No fishing, no wading, no swimming."

Daniel stopped. "Ellie, this next part sounds so far-fetched, so…so strange." He searched her face. "But I swear it's true."

"You got what you deserved, I [illegible]e it."

"More than I deserved," he said ro[illegible]hly, and scowled.

Ellie's thoughts blipped to the tiki i[illegible]he Kamehanas' back garden.

"The driver stopped on the pavement a[illegible]e filed out to walk to the beach. There was a full mo[illegible]nd I was entranced. Imagine a postcard of a South S[illegible]land—palm trees swaying, the moon creating a hig[illegible] to itself over the water. And I wanted to swim[illegible] that highway more than I wanted anything in my li[illegible]

His voice held such anguish that Ellie touched his[illegible]d.

"I was spellbound," he whispered. "Literally."

He cleared his throat. "The cove was the last stop[illegible] the tour, but I refused to get back on the bus. I'd ma[illegible] my own way back to Honolulu, I told the guide."

His laugh held no humor. "Don't ask me how I thought I would do that with Honolulu on the other side of the mountains and me on foot, but I was beyond caring. All I could think of was that beckoning moonlight."

Looking down, Ellie was surprised to see that she'd taken Daniel's hand. Or perhaps he'd taken hers. She felt a faint tremor in his fingers.

"Then everyone was gone and I was alone on the beach. There was a sign. Danger No Swimming Stay Out Of The Water. Didn't apply to me, I thought. I'm a good swimmer, and the guide hadn't said anything about sharks. He just said the old ones didn't like sharing their turf. Hell, I was a Morgan. There wasn't a fine too steep. I shucked down to my underwear and waded in."

He sent her an absent, meaningless smile. "I forgot about my money belt."

His voice dropped. "The water was like nothing I'd ever felt. Liquid moonlight is the nearest I can describe it. I started swimming…."

The hand around hers had a definite grip now. Ellie couldn't bring herself to look at him.

"And the moonlight disappeared," he said. "Everything disappeared. I thought I was drowning. And maybe I did. I'm not sure anymore. Something sucked me so far down… There was no *me* anymore. No anything. Only a voice. 'You must learn,' it said. Maybe it said."

Again Daniel cleared his throat, as if words had been clogging it for years. "Or maybe I just felt the voice. I don't know. Then I woke up in the Kamehanas' back garden. Not that I'm completely sure it's reality."

This time Ellie looked at him. "You're saying that their backyard isn't real? Daniel, you must have hit your head or something—"

"Their garden is very real, Ellie," Daniel said with a laugh. "I'm not sure *I'm* the reality."

"You've lost me."

He blew out a frustrated breath. "Now you know how I feel."

"You're breathing," Ellie said.

"Yeah, guess I am."

"And you can talk."

He nodded.

"You can move."

He kissed her knuckles.

"You can kiss," she whispered. "I think you're real."

And his mouth claimed hers, holding everything in the world that Ellie wanted, and she knew Daniel's yearning matched her own.

Still, it was he who drew away.

He kissed her forehead. "Ellie, I'm *not* real. I can't be. Even though I can do all the things you said, what I can't do is control myself."

"You seem to be managing pretty darn well," Ellie replied tartly. Her body still zinged.

She'd forgotten the fiancée in this story.

So what was she doing kissing an engaged man? For that matter, what was he doing kissing her?

She stood.

And Daniel stood with her but was careful not to touch her, she noticed. Okay, fine.

"I'm tired and I want to go to bed," she said. "We'll pick this conversation up at a later date, if we pick it up at all. I want you to leave now."

This time he knew better than to argue.

"Of course. But before I go, I want to say how much I appreciate you listening to me tonight. I've wanted to tell someone for so long—"

"Yeah, I'm a good listener. Good night."

Would the man just *leave!* If he kept talking she was going to cry again. Heaven knew why.

"Good night."

He angled toward the street as she turned and half ran toward the apartment.

Tonight was something for the books. She'd talked about LeAnne for the first time since...well, for the first time. She'd cried. She'd been kissed by a master kisser.

Sliding the patio door open, Ellie entered the dim kitchen where Chad had left the light over the sink on for her. Taking off Gram's silver earrings, she rubbed her earlobes before drawing a glass of water.

Thinking of Gram made her remember Daniel's tale—part of a tale, because he hadn't finished it. Not that she could have stood much more of the man tonight. Still, his story sounded like something straight from her own family chronicles.

The thought had her half strangling on a sip of water.

Caught up in the strangeness of his story, she'd completely forgotten Daniel was supposed to explain why he was following her.

Okay. Not exactly following her. "Forced to hang around," that was it.

Hang around, my aunt Fanny! The man darn sure better be gone.

Marching over to the patio door, she slid it open and checked.

The side lawn, illuminated with moonlight, held not so much as a shadow. Only a sleepy night bird disturbed its silence. Daniel was nowhere in sight.

Caught between relief and disappointment, Ellie slid the door closed again and locked it, then padded back to the sink to flip off the kitchen light.

Daniel settled in, accepting the jolt of nothingness he always received when the wood first closed around him. He was getting used to it.

His prison was never uncomfortable, and he felt no restraints. In the state he was in, he needed absolutely nothing. Not warmth, nor air, nor sustenance or shelter.

But now Ellie Simms had come on the scene and, for whatever reason, when she was around he could be himself—his new self.

The spoiled rich kid who wound up in the waters of the cove didn't exist anymore.

And he *had* been a kid. Almost thirty but without a clue. Sure he'd been to medical school and to Europe, called congressmen for lunch and movie stars for impulsive trips to the Caribbean.

Been everywhere, done everything.

But all he really *understood* was money and which fork to use. He didn't know a thing about how the world worked if it didn't impact on him or his fortune.

Then he went for that fateful swim.

With the Morgan millions having nothing to buy during his years of confinement, he was forced to search for another means of identity. It was that or go insane.

Strangely, he found that identity in the knowledge of medicine Nona sometimes let him practice. While running a clinic catering to a wealthy clientele no longer held appeal, practicing medicine for those who really needed him did.

Would Laura like the man he'd become? Four years was a long time. Had she waited?

He doubted it on both counts. Still, her family wanted the Morgan connection as badly as his wanted the Neubauer connection. And while practicing in the Hamptons wasn't what he wanted anymore, there were his parents to consider. He *was* a Morgan, and he supposed the rich could be just as sick as the poor.

Had his family declared him dead? Technically, he supposed, he was still a missing person. But, hell, he'd gone dancing! Quite a feat for a corpse.

And he was doing it again at the first opportunity. With Ellie, who fit in his arms as if she was made for them, and who danced with him as if she was the music itself.

Was she married? She'd lost a child. Was there a husband at home? God, he hoped not.

Ellie dreamed of LeAnne and woke in the middle of the night. Sitting up against the pillows, she touched her still-smiling lips. Oh, she thought in wonder. Oh.

Beautiful LeAnne. Precious LeAnne. Smelling of baby and delight. Silky-soft skin and rolls of baby fat. A chortle, truly somewhere between a chuckle and a gurgle, that could make Ellie laugh after the most horrid workday.

What a gift her baby was. Apparently put on earth on short-term loan, but how *chosen* she felt to be LeAnne's mother for the baby's brief stay.

Ellie's eyes drifted shut, her smile still in place....

As the night sky paled and pinkened into dawn, Daniel watched the stars blink out one by one.

Would he see Ellie today? he wondered. He hoped so. Hope. Something he hadn't felt in a long time.

Though still chained to the Kamehanas' back garden,

now he was also chained to a woman made of moonlight. It could be worse.

It *had* been worse.

Now there was hope. Now there was Ellie.

Ellie woke again with a snort and a scowl in the small hours of the morning.

Daniel Morgan, she thought balefully, *what are you doing in my dreams?*

Kissing you, she imagined him answering. *And very thoroughly, I might add.*

Well, you can just stop it!

Reaching out, Ellie flipped on the bedside lamp.

Not only did she dream of Daniel kissing her, but she'd dreamed of thoroughly kissing him back. That was the good part.

The bad part was she woke up remembering what she'd been thinking when he kissed her in reality.

That Daniel's lips held everything in the world that she wanted.

No! she thought now, grabbing her mouth. No, no, no, no, *no!*

Not Daniel. Not any man. She had a job to do, a life plan that didn't include getting locked into someone else's expectations. Never again.

Okay. Chad was right. Her family was right. She needed to play sometime.

But the operative word here was *play*. It was not getting sidetracked by a few moonlight kisses. It was not letting Da—make that any man—steer her away from her goal.

It was not letting Da—any man into her heart.

* * *

When Chad got up the following morning, Ellie was already sitting at the kitchen table eating a bowl of cereal.

"You're up early," he said, yawning and scratching his chest.

"Um."

"And talkative."

Her brother poured himself a cup of coffee and a glass of orange juice, then filled a small mixing bowl full of cereal and milk before he, too, sat down at the table.

He glanced at her. "Guess you're all talked out after last night." Even with a mouth full of Fruity O's he managed a leer.

"Don't be ridiculous."

"What? You didn't learn Daniel's life story?"

"Only to the part where he went swimming where he shouldn't. That came after the part where his fiancée flew home to plan their wedding."

"Ah."

He went back to studiously chewing his cereal.

Ellie knew the signs. "Give," she ordered. "What do you know about him?"

"I dunno. What do you know?"

Had her brother not been six foot three and with the brawn to match his profession, her look would have pinned him to the wall.

"Let me put it another way. If you don't tell me what's going on, Charles Chadwick Simms, you'll come home this afternoon to find every pair of underwear you own with the seat ripped out."

Chad grabbed his rump with both hands. "No, please! Anything but that! I give! Here's everything I know." He lifted the pitcher. "Orange juice?"

Doing her best to look mean and determined while fighting a laugh, Ellie shook her head. "I'm waiting."

"The marines need you, woman. We'd have all the enemy's secrets in no time."

"Don't change the subject."

"Right. Daniel Morgan is a medical doctor but he's not afraid to inflict a little pain for a just cause. He chews with his mouth closed, gets a real kick out of some really strange things, and he's hiding something."

"What is he hiding?"

"That I *don't* know. I figured you would by now. Especially after last night."

Ellie strove for patience. "You know why he's 'forced to hang around,' Chad, and I want to know why, too."

Her brother was no fool. He dropped the banter. "No, El, I don't know *why.* I just know that he is, and that he has no control over it."

No control. Daniel had used the same phrase.

"But I *can* tell you this," Chad continued, leaving the table to take his dishes to the sink before facing her.

"I trust him, Sissy, and I think he's a good man."

Slowly Ellie nodded. Her brother only called her Sissy when he was dead serious.

He'd told her all he knew.

Chad left the kitchen but she remained at the table, nursing a last cup of coffee.

When he returned, he was dressed to go on post. With his cammies ironed and sharp, his pant legs folded neatly into his spotlessly shined boots, and his "cover," as he called his cap, sitting squarely atop his shorn head, he looked the epitome of a U.S. fighting man who was all business.

But to Ellie he was simply her little brother. Good thing he didn't have big ears, she thought and kissed him on the cheek.

"You are so cute," she said, giving him a saccharine smile. "Have a good day."

He snorted. "In the marines? You gotta be kiddin'. I should be home early. We'll do something."

But as he turned away, Chad spied Ellie's earrings on the cabinet where she'd left them last night. Picking them up, he hooked them into her earlobes.

"You have a good day, too, El," he said.

She laughed up at him and shook her head, making the earrings jiggle a bit. "You really like these things, don't you?"

But his answering grin was sweetness itself. "You seem happy when you wear them," he replied gently, only to turn on the Texas drawl because he knew it irritated her. "Prob'bly 'cause they're so sexy." And he winked.

Ellie rolled her eyes.

"They're pretty on you, El," her brother added in his natural voice. "Gram knows how to pick 'em. Later, gator." And he was gone.

Chapter Eight

What should she do today? Ellie stepped into a pair of shorts, then pulled a V-neck, sleeveless, knit shirt over her head. Would she see Daniel?

She shook her head. Cancel that.

As she gazed at herself in the mirror to catch her hair into a loose ponytail, the earrings Chad placed in earlobes caught the early-morning sunlight.

Maybe she'd take TheBus into Honolulu. Or back to Waikiki. She'd seen some interesting shops the other night. A necklace to match Gram's earrings would be nice. She might even give it to Gram.

Funny how Chad was so hung up on these earrings. She'd never known her brother to notice jewelry of any kind, but he certainly liked her silver flowers.

It was probably their link to Gram. He didn't say it,

but her brother was homesick and it would be another year before he got back to Texas.

The Simmses were a close-knit family. Ellie couldn't imagine growing up like Daniel had, without cousins and aunts and uncles popping in and out of her personal business. Sure there were spats and jealousies and gossip, but there was also love and generosity of spirit.

Poor Daniel.

Poor Daniel, nothing! Ellie puffed out a disgusted breath. The man would *not* be a part of her day today.

So naturally she found him sitting at the picnic table when she opened the patio door.

Good holy grief.

Determined not to notice how the early-morning sun picked out the blond highlights in his pale hair, she marched over so she could glare at close range. "Scram. Or else, buster. I mean it!"

He didn't so much as bat an eyelash, just looked beleaguered. "Ellie, I *can't.* I tried to tell you that last night."

"You left last night," Ellie told him coldly. "I checked."

"Yeah, but I don't know how I did it."

"One foot in front of the other probably. You can practice now."

If anything, he looked even more put upon. "Uh, no. I've tried that. One foot in front of the other doesn't do it. I get stopped every time."

"Mmm-hmm. So how did you manage last night?"

"I, uh…well, it was a…*phhtt.*"

"A what? I didn't catch that."

"A *phhtt,*" Daniel repeated. "One second I'm here, and the next second I'm not. You know, *phhtt!*"

"My name isn't Alice, and this ain't Wonderland," Ellie said coldly. "What the heck are you talking about?"

He scowled right back at her. "That's what I'm trying to tell you. I don't *know* what the heck I'm talking about!"

His scowl seemed familiar.

"Just listen to me, would you? When I can finally leave, I'm just gone. I don't walk away. I don't run or fly or swim. I'm just not here anymore. In the blink of an eye, I'm somewhere else."

That silenced her. Ellie stared at Daniel for a long moment, then slowly sat down on the bench beside him.

"Where are you?"

"In the Kamehanas' back garden."

"What?"

"What I said. I'm in the Kamehanas' back garden. I told you I woke up there after I swam in the cove, remember? And that's where I've been ever since. Until now."

"You've been with the Kamehanas for *four years?*" Ellie exclaimed. "*Why,* for Heaven's sake?"

"I didn't say I was living with them. I said I was in their back garden."

She gaped. "The Kamehanas are holding you *prisoner?*"

"No! Yes. I mean, of course not. Not the Kamehanas. But something, Ellie. I don't know how to explain it. All I know is that when I'm not with you, I can't leave Tom and Janie's back garden."

"You're locked up?"

"Not...exactly." He sighed again. "Thank God it's you I'm talking to. Anyone else would think if I'm *not* locked up, I ought to be."

That wasn't what Ellie wanted to hear.

"What makes me so special?" she asked, trying to make her voice cold and aloof, when actually the simple question carried an urgency she didn't understand.

Daniel shrugged but sent her a brief smile. "You said weird things happened in your family, too," he said.

Good answer. A reasonable answer. Logical. So why did she feel so dissatisfied?

Leaning back, Daniel watched a bright-colored bird flit through the shrubbery lining the apartment house. "I'm not locked up, but I'm...in something, actually a part of something near the family's back fence. A tree, I think."

Ellie stared at him. "Even my family doesn't get *this* weird."

"It gets weirder. Because, Ellie, now there's you."

She shook her head. "Uh-uh, there isn't."

"Uh-huh, there is. For whatever reason, when I'm...released...it's only to you. *Phhtt,* here I am. And I can't leave. Like I said, I can only get so far away from you and that's it."

Everything in Ellie rebelled against that little piece of information. "Prove it," she said, glaring at him. "Walk."

With a sideways ironic bow, Daniel walked. He got as far as the apartment drive when to all appearances he ran into something.

"This is it," he called. To demonstrate, he leaned at such an impossible angle he should have fallen off balance. He even turned around, placed his hands against the air, went up on his toes, and did slanted push-ups off it....

Falling flat when Ellie left the picnic table and walked toward him.

She held out a hand to give him a hoist up and looked around. "Quite a show, but I don't see anything."

"I don't, either," Daniel replied, swiping dirt off his rear. "I just feel it. At any rate, it's not here anymore." He waved vaguely. "Now it's over there somewhere. You moved."

At her look, Daniel heaved a long-suffering sigh.

"It's *you,* Ellie. Don't you get it? For whatever reason, you hold my leash. I can only go so far from wherever you are and then I'm stopped. When you move, the wall, or whatever it is, moves too."

Caught by the truth in his eyes, Ellie stared back at him, until she realized she was also caught by how very attractive his blue eyes were.

She blinked. Uh-uh.

Turning on her heel, she started walking.

Behind her, Daniel muttered something unpleasant. "So where are we going?" he asked bitterly, following her.

"To the cove."

When he halted, she didn't turn around. She didn't stop, either.

"Ellie, no! Haven't you heard anything I've said? The place is dangerous."

"Not to me. I'm not the one who went swimming in it."

"All right, I was stupid. But not stupid enough to be stupid twice."

"So I should hope. Make sure you stay out of the water this time."

She kept walking. "According to you, the cove is what started this mess you've somehow drawn me into, and I want to see what it looks like. In the daylight."

Daniel growled and swore and muttered, but he trailed after her until his long strides caught up with her shorter ones and then he walked beside her.

"I hope you know what you're doing," he said at last.

Ellie didn't. But going to the cove was all she knew to do. She hoped Daniel was as afraid as she was.

Not afraid of the cove, of course. All one had to do was stay out of the water. The sign said so, and with her background, Ellie believed in signs.

What frightened her was the control Daniel had over her. He might bemoan the fact that he *had* to be with her, but that was nothing. A little kink in the universe.

The real clunker in Ellie's up-to-now orderly world was that she *wanted* to be with him. She'd been fighting that fact since the first night on the beach.

What was wrong with her?

The cove started it. Maybe it could explain it.

At least there her fear and Daniel's would be equal. His of the elements; hers of her heart.

When Daniel caught up with Ellie, he breathed a sigh of relief. Not that walking behind her was a hardship. That was the problem.

Watching those long legs of hers eat up the distance

made him want to catch her in his arms and do a little nibbling of his own.

Was she married? he wondered for the thousandth time. She wore no ring, but many nurses didn't.

The idea of Ellie being married made him a little sick to his stomach. He didn't know why. In the situation he was in, whether or not a woman was married certainly had no bearing on anything.

Or maybe he did know why. He planned to kiss Ellie Simms again at the first promising moment and he'd never been someone who played around with married women.

But he'd already kissed her once and found it wasn't enough. He wanted more. The heck of it was, he was beginning to think he wasn't playing.

When she kissed him last night was it just because she was vulnerable and he an available guy on a tropical night?

"Available" being an iffy word, of course.

So caught up in his thoughts was he that they were halfway across the sand before Daniel realized they were at the cove.

He stopped, grabbing Ellie's arm.

"We're not getting any closer," he said firmly.

Ellie being Ellie, she looked at his hand on her arm then pointedly looked into his face.

"I mean it," he said.

And he did. If he had to wrestle the woman to the ground, he would, but he'd be damned if she was getting any nearer to water that carried who knew what in its depths.

"I am going," she told him, "to that tree over there.

You can sit in the sun if you want, but I'm finding some shade."

Oh. Feeling sheepish, Daniel dropped her arm. She was right. He was the one who'd been stupid here.

Knowing Ellie wasn't thrilled with his presence, at the moment, Daniel took a spot a little away from her when she plopped down on the sand in the shade of the tamarisk tree. He wasn't all that thrilled himself.

Sure he wanted to kiss her. More than kiss her. And he loved being around her, talking, laughing…dancing.

It felt so damn good being a part of this woman's world. At the moment he couldn't think of a place he'd rather be. But he hated having no choice.

Still, enjoy the moment, he thought. And he would. As soon as he cleared something up.

"Are you married, Ellie?"

She looked at him, clearly startled. "Not anymore."

His heart gave a little gurgle of satisfaction.

"Are you still engaged?" she asked.

And it was his turn to be startled. "I don't know. Maybe. Guess it depends on how long Laura was willing to wait without seeing the body."

He kept his tone flippant, hoping to dismiss the subject. Laura came from a planet far far away, from a time long long ago. He didn't want to talk about her.

Ellie did. "She was probably devastated when you disappeared," she said softly. "And your family must be grief stricken."

Giving it another try, Daniel shrugged slightly. "It was at least four years ago, Ellie. I imagine everyone's over it by now."

"Not your mother."

Her voice was so quiet and sad and sure that in spite of himself, Daniel moved closer so he could take her hand. He kissed her knuckles.

His mother probably hadn't missed a bridge game, Daniel thought, once it was a certainty her son wouldn't be found. The Morgans were famous for their stiff upper lips.

A polite way of saying they just didn't give a damn as long as their own lives weren't disrupted.

"Daniel," Ellie asked after a moment, "why me?"

"I don't know," he replied, knowing what she meant. "But I'm grateful. I'm hoping, now you've shaken things up, the *whatever* will forgive me and set me free."

"In all the time you've been in…in the Kamehanas' back garden no one else has ever, er, shaken things up?"

"No one. Not exactly, anyway. There's always been a glimmer of something when Nona puts a plumeria lei around my neck," he added slowly.

"I thought you were a tree."

Daniel laughed. "Hell, Ellie, I don't know what I am. Think about it. I can't see myself, I can only see out. But when Nona hangs plumeria leis somewhere near me or puts them on the ground in front of me, we can sort of communicate, she and I."

"The flower of Hawaii," Ellie murmured. "How do you and Nona communicate?"

Rubbing a hand over his mouth, Daniel knew the more he tried to explain, the sillier he sounded.

"Mentally, I suppose," he said, "but only when she brings the plumerias."

Ellie didn't laugh, bless her. "What do you, um, talk about?"

"Not politics, that's for sure. Nona never wants anything from me but my services as a doctor."

Now Ellie really did look startled. "She thinks you're a god?"

"Bite your tongue. Nona's a good Presbyterian. She's also a gifted herbalist. Still, when she's unsure about what's ailing one of the children, she…she asks me."

Loaded with a nurse's common sense, Ellie didn't say a word. She didn't have to.

Daniel shook his head reprovingly. "Not even close," he said. Hell, he was an M.D., not a witch doctor.

"She relates the symptoms, tells me what she thinks is wrong, and I either confirm or question her opinion. After that, she takes the child to the doctor if one or both of us thinks it's necessary."

Holding Ellie's gaze with his own, he made his point. "She goes to a physician capable of doing an extensive examination, not one who lives in a tree and has to guess based on secondhand information."

Ellie considered that a moment. "All right, let's get back to me," she said at last.

"I like coming back to you."

Though she shot him a telling look, he'd noticed a small, sweet tilt in the corner of her mouth when she was amused. He enjoyed watching for it.

Soon he would kiss her just there.

"The first time I saw you was at this cove," she said. "What could I have done to bring you here that night? I certainly didn't hang any plumeria leis around your neck."

Mention of the cove sent a frisson up Daniel's backbone. This woman had a gift for killing a tender moment.

"I don't know," he replied. Every time he opened his mouth, he thought, that phrase popped out.

"I just remember suddenly being here. *Phhtt.* And seeing you ready to walk into the water. You scared the hell out of me that night. Once I knew you weren't going to do anything silly, though, I thought you the most beautiful woman I'd ever seen."

Ellie didn't seem at all impressed by the compliment, though he'd meant it with every fiber of his being.

"Mmm-hmm," she said. But he noticed the tiny crease playing around her mouth again.

"You scared the hell out of *me* that night," she added, gazing at him through her lashes.

Daniel wanted to laugh. Other parts of his body wanted something else.

"Once I knew you weren't into anything silly, I thought you were kinda pretty, too. Maybe too pretty, Beach Boy Bob."

He grinned and hiked a brow. "But you wanted to kiss me."

"You wanted to kiss *me*."

"Yeah, I did. Like I want to kiss you right now," he admitted softly. "I didn't get a chance then. You sent me away."

"No," Ellie whispered. "I didn't...."

Daniel's hands cupped her face just under her jaw, tilting her face to his. And then he kissed her.

Oh, Ellie thought, and sighed, her breath whispering into his mouth. Oh.

She'd wanted it, blatantly asked for it. And now she received it.

And now she was lost.

Daniel's lips found each corner of her mouth, his tongue teasing there a moment and making her smile.

Was that triumph she heard in his low, husky laugh? But his mouth had already traveled on to explore other parts of her face, finding nerve endings she'd forgotten existed before it homed in on her lips once again.

Yes, she was lost. And she was loving it.

She wanted more. Please more.

But Daniel pulled away and stared at her in horror.

"Oh, God, Ellie. Don't cry. I'm so sorry."

As she stared up at him blankly, his thumbs brushed away tears she'd been completely unaware of.

"No," she said, stopping him simply by cupping her two hands over his, which were still bracketing her face. "It's not you. It's me. Daniel, I…"

One of her earrings bounced off their paired hands and dropped to the sand.

Ellie laughed damply. "Just like the first ti—"

She stared.

Daniel's face, looking startled and disoriented, wavered in front of her.

Trying to clear her vision, Ellie blinked rapidly.

But it wasn't her at all…it was *him!*

His hands, beneath hers and still cupping her face, felt like ice.

"Daniel? *Daniel!* Lie down. Quickly!"

Alarmed, Ellie tried to push him from his sitting position so he could lie on the sand, but he shook his head, his hands dropping from her face—a small movement that made him even more insubstantial.

Ellie gasped. She could see right through him.

But fear turned to fierce protective anger. *You can't have him, dammit. He's mine!*

Making a grab for Daniel's misty outline, she shifted to her knees, ready to hang on and never let go...and was jabbed in her kneecap.

When she dropped a hand to brush whatever it was away, she found the rough shape of her earring. Without thought, Ellie snatched it up, thrust it through her earlobe, and wrapped her arms fully around Daniel, holding him for dear life.

His shoulders and trunk filled her arms, their mass substantial and hard. His heart beat a strong tattoo beneath her cheek; erratic, yes, but pumping life for all it was worth.

Ellie closed her eyes and clung. If Daniel disappeared now, he was taking her with him.

Nothing happened.

She opened her eyes.

They were still on the beach, and Daniel was solid within her embrace, as she was in his.

Taking a deep breath, Ellie leaned back and risked looking up at him....

His smile at her might be a little shaky, but it was there. And he might look a little dazed, but his face had lines to it again.

Pulling away for a better look, but hanging on to a wrist just in case, Ellie gave him a professional once-over. The woman in her liked what she saw, and the nurse in her did, too.

He looked pale, but his color was already returning. The pulse beneath her fingers beat satisfactorily.

Because she liked the feel of it, Ellie shifted her hand so that Daniel's pulse beat against her palm.

He used his other hand to swipe across mouth. "Sorry. Don't know what happened there. I felt a little sick for a minute."

"Is that the way you feel when you, um, disappear?"

"A little. But it's usually quick. *Phhtt,* you know."

His wobbly grin was so gallant it was all Ellie could do not to wrap the man in her arms again.

"But then I'm back in my tree," he continued. "This kind of thing isn't usual at all."

Ellie thought about it. "Maybe because it wasn't a complete *phhtt.* This time you only half disappeared."

"I did?"

She nodded. "I think you need to go back to Chad's apartment and get out of the sun for a while. You're looking a little peaked."

"You just said I was pretty," Daniel replied, standing with her, his grin stronger now, and his eyes gleaming with mischief.

"I've changed my mind."

Pretty, Ellie thought, disgusted with her vocabulary. Such a nonword. What had she been thinking? *Sexy,* now, had a ring to it. *Yummy.* That one wasn't bad.

On a sharp breath, she reined in drifting thoughts.

Dangerous was the word.

How the heck was she going to get rid of this man she never wanted to let go of again?

When he placed a casual arm around her shoulders, it was all she could do not to shrug out from under it.

And all she could do not to turn more into it.

So Daniel's sheltering arm remained, and she simply accepted it.

But halfway across the sand to the street, he stopped. "Wait a minute, would you? I want to look. I've never seen this place in the daylight, either."

So the two of them stood for a moment, and Daniel gazed across the sand at the beach, now being sweetly kissed by an ocean impossibly blue.

A beautiful spot, Ellie thought. Peaceful. Serene.

The sun, high overhead, glinted off wavelets creating miniflashes of gold.

Down the beach, a mother sat with her two toddlers and watched them build a sand castle.

Ellie watched them, too, for a moment. The group looked Hawaiian, the mother obviously not worried. She probably understood the cove's limits and would pass that understanding on to her children.

"Hard to believe that hell can be so beautiful." Daniel said quietly.

But Ellie, too, understood limits. "If you held your breath till you passed out, would you blame your body for being weak?" she asked just as quietly.

Under his arm she felt him go still.

"Point taken. Shall we go?"

* * *

Back at Chad's apartment, Ellie made tuna salad for lunch, while Daniel prowled the living area of the apartment's open floor plan. He picked things up and put them down without looking at them, a far cry from his usual fascination and sensory delight in everything.

The sandwiches, chips and soda they had for lunch didn't seem to have much appeal, either.

Ellie doubted he tasted them. She didn't.

Looking up, she caught Daniel staring at her. When their eyes met, something zinged between them. Ellie's heart flipped, and Daniel looked startled.

Fumbling her chair back from the table, Ellie stood and hurried from the room.

She came back carrying her cell phone.

"Okay, E.T.," she said evenly, holding it out to him. "Call home."

Daniel looked at the small phone as if were a dirty scalpel. "And say what?" he asked hoarsely, not touching it.

"You'll think of something." Whether he liked it or not, Ellie thrust the instrument into his hands. "You have to tell your parents you're not dead. It's not fair to put them through this."

Daniel looked at her, then back at the phone sitting like a small turtle in his palm. He opened it slowly, as if expecting it to snap.

"Just punch in the number, Daniel."

Taking a deep breath, Daniel punched in the series of numbers and put the phone to his ear.

Ellie stood to leave the room and give him privacy.

He grabbed her hand. “Don’t you dare,” he whispered.

Keeping his gaze pinned on her, he spoke into the phone. “Hello, Mz. J?”

The housekeeper, he mouthed.

“Mz. J, this is Daniel. Yes, it’s me. C’mon, J-J, don’t cry. I’m fine. Yes, I’m sure.”

He was silent a moment, listening, his face a study of softness and worry. After a moment his gaze left Ellie’s and shifted to the floor.

“Mz. J, I have to talk to my mother now,” he said gently. “Would you call her, please?”

Chapter Nine

Daniel waited as Mrs. Johnson put him through to his mother's office. He'd never been inside the Kamehanas' home, of course, but he doubted Nona or Janie had an office where they handled their social lives.

"Daniel?"

"Yes, Mother. I wanted to tell you I was all right."

"I know that," she replied. "Why has it taken you this long to call? Your father and I were worried."

"I'm…in a situation where I couldn't call. How did you know I wasn't… That is, how did you know I was alive?"

"Not from you, obviously," his mother snapped. "You used your credit card a few days ago. We were notified. The signatures matched. Your scrawl isn't easily duplicated. What situation?"

"It's, ah, difficult to explain. I'm still in Hawaii. I guess you know that. But I can't come home. My situation is such that I…that is…"

"You're doing something with the FBI, aren't you?" his mother broke in coldly.

"FBI?"

"If not the FBI, then the CIA. Daniel, I'm not an idiot. Of course we knew you were not dead. The Hawaiian police couldn't find a body, and couldn't explain why you might have drowned in such shallow water when you've been an excellent swimmer since you were five. They hemmed and hawed, saying some things couldn't be explained."

"Some things *can't* be explained," Daniel tried to insert.

This whole conversation bordered on the surreal. Holding Ellie's gaze and more than willing to get lost in their blue depths, he listened as his mother denied everything he'd just said.

Just as she'd been doing his whole life.

"Everything is explainable. Now I want you home immediately. It was bad enough when you decided to become a doctor, but Morgans do not spy, or whatever agents do."

"Mother, I'm not… Never mind," he said tiredly. He gripped Ellie's hand. "Um, how is Laura?"

"Laura? Why she's— How do you think she is?" his mother snapped. "She's hurt, of course. As you can imagine with the wedding only a few weeks away when you disappeared, then having to face her friends. How could you, Daniel? How *could* you?"

Not easily, Daniel thought. "I didn't mean to hurt anyone, Mother," he said aloud. "Is she seeing someone else now?"

There was a tiny pause. "Not everyone is as unreliable as you have chosen to be, young man. Your father is appalled, as am I. As for Laura, she is waiting for you to come home and do the right thing."

Daniel felt his heart turn to lead. "Tell her not to wait," he said urgently. "I don't know how long it will be before I can leave here. I promise you, it's not my decision to make."

"Well then, your father has connections. Very important connections. He'll have you terminated from this situation at once. Whom shall he call?"

"I told you, Mother. This isn't anything that can be handled that way. I'm sorry. I..."

"Being sorry carries no weight in this matter, Daniel. Laura is waiting. Your father and I are waiting. Stop whatever it is you think you are doing at once and come home to your responsibilities. Your father is not well. If he were not playing golf this afternoon, he would tell you this himself."

In spite of how sick he felt, Daniel almost laughed. "Mother, I—"

"You will do the right thing, Daniel, and you will do it at once. You're a Morgan. Goodbye."

His mother broke the connection, but Daniel held the phone to his ear for a second or two longer. "Goodbye," he finally said, and didn't recognize his own voice.

He handed the instrument to Ellie.

At one time the conversation he'd just had with his

mother would have been nothing unusual to him. Morgans, after all, deemed emotional display quite vulgar. He'd thought all families did.

But that was before he'd spent years surrounded by the exuberant delight the Kamehanas found in each other.

Now when Ellie hurled herself into his arms with a small cry, it was all he could do not to bawl with her.

"I'm so sorry," she whispered into his neck. "Daniel, I'm so sorry."

He swallowed, unable to speak, and held on to her for dear life.

Ellie clutched Daniel as close as she could get him. She hadn't heard the whole conversation, but she'd heard Daniel's half of it. Based on nothing but his rigidly neutral face as he'd talked with her, his mother—mother, hah!—deserved to flunk parent school.

The only person to show any emotion at all over the fact that he wasn't dead was the housekeeper. No wonder he'd been reluctant to call his parents.

Yet here he was, tenderly rubbing his hands up and down her back, making shushing noises. Trying to comfort *her,* she thought incredulously, as she felt his lips brush her hair.

She cried even harder. Didn't his mother realize what a fine man he was?

"Hush, Ellie," Daniel whispered. "It's not that bad. You don't miss what you've never had."

Ellie snorted, giving the statement the response it deserved.

Drawing out of Daniel's arms, she took his face in her

two hands so she could look into his eyes. "Yes, you do," she said firmly. "But they're the losers, Daniel, not you."

He smiled wryly. "A moot point, wouldn't you say? My parents are my parents, Ellie, and they're all I've got. They're who they were trained to be, you know, and if I'm ever free of...this, I'll go home and be a Morgan, too."

Taking one of her hands, he kissed the inside of her fingers. "Any iced tea left?"

End of subject, Ellie thought. And after all, what could she say?

Rubbing her hands over her face, she wiped away the useless tears and dried her cheeks. That the process included passing the fingers Daniel had just kissed over her lips was mere coincidence.

"I think so," she replied, striving to keep her voice equally light. "I promised Chad a pie while I was here. He's leaving in a few days and so am I, so I think I'll be Susie Homemaker today. Wanna help?"

When Chad came home that afternoon, the smell of apple pie met him at the door. To keep herself busy, Ellie even baked a batch of chocolate chip cookies.

Her baby brother was nothing if not steeped in American tradition, she thought fondly when he swung her around in gratitude.

And thank goodness for Chad's laughing presence to brighten an atmosphere growing more and more somber between her and Daniel throughout the afternoon.

After Daniel's disastrous conversation with his mother, the two of them had to work hard to keep things light.

Being chatty as she never had before in her life, Ellie brought Daniel up to date on various events taking place on the mainland that he hadn't heard about. She even instigated a heated argument when she discovered he was a New Jersey Nets fan. Everyone knew the San Antonio Spurs were the best team in the NBA.

Oh, the two of them chattered away like magpies.

And should silence sneak in and become too comfortable, Daniel found a question to ask or she found a comment to make.

Silence, each of them knew, led straight to danger.

To thoughts of Laura, for instance. The fiancée who waited.

Or to Ellie's return to the mainland.

But now Chad kept them laughing, adding a third person to the mix and giving them someone else to talk to. Around Chad, silence didn't stand a chance.

Her brother was no fool, however. "Looks like going to town tonight isn't an option," he said, eyeing them both knowingly, "So how about heading over to the pizza place for supper, then coming back and having Ellie's apple pie for dessert?"

A good plan.

All of them wanted to change before going out. Chad to get out of his work clothes, Ellie to freshen up, and Daniel to change into yet another pair of Chad's shorts and T-shirts.

With clothes and showers a nonissue for Daniel most of the time, when he was…out…he liked being fresh.

Perhaps he and Ellie could go shopping, he thought, as he stood under the shower and reveled in the feel of hot water pelting his chest and back. Neither the casual style of Hawaii, nor Chad's spartan lifestyle—which

Daniel was now a part of—called for the wardrobe he'd worn back home. But he would like his own things.

Mindful that Chad wanted to shower, too, Daniel stepped out of the cubicle, quickly toweled off and hustled into another pair of shorts. Ellie's brother had even found him a pair of flip-flops, another mainstay of the islands.

He was pulling a bright red T-shirt over his head when it happened.

Phhht.

Well, damn.

Ellie emerged from her bedroom wearing a fresh pair of shorts and a tropical print blouse that wrapped around and tied just under her breasts.

She'd left her hair long and loose.

In the hall she found Chad standing impatiently outside the bathroom. "Get a move on, bud," he called through the closed door.

When he saw Ellie, he grinned. "Lookin' good there, El," he said, but returned his attention to the bathroom door. "Hey, I'm hungry, man! Hustle it up."

No answer.

Frowning, Chad glanced at Ellie, then looked again.

She wondered if she had dirt on her nose.

"Are you wearing your earrings, El?"

Ellie rolled her eyes. "No. And I'm not putting them on, either. I can't wear them all the time, Chad. They're too heavy. I've had them in all day and my ears hurt. Besides, you can't see them under my hair."

Her brother considered that a moment. "Guess not,"

he said, sounding disappointed. Giving the knob a token rattle, he opened the door.

"Looks like our guest flew the coop."

"What!"

Peering in herself, Ellie surveyed the small bathroom, its air heavy with moisture and smelling of soap and Chad's deodorant. A damp towel hung over a rack, and the clothes Daniel had worn lay in a heap on the floor.

With the door to the shower stall standing open, there was absolutely no place anyone could hide.

Not that Daniel was hiding. This time Ellie hadn't been there to hold him.

But *this time* she knew where he was.

"I made cookies this afternoon," she told Chad abruptly, turning away from the empty bathroom. "I think I'll take some to the Kamehanas."

"Hey, I thought you made those for me," her brother protested.

"You can share," she told him heartlessly. "Back in a few."

Armed with a plate of cookies, Ellie knocked on the Kamehanas' door.

Georgie answered it, sending her his gap-toothed smile in the process.

Though she had other things on her mind, Ellie grinned back. "Hi, Georgie. Is Nona here?"

Without taking his eyes or his smile from Ellie, the little boy yelled, "Noooonaaa!"

"I'm here, Georgie. No need to bellow," the old woman said mildly, coming up behind him. She, too, smiled at Ellie, appearing not at all surprised to see a visitor this late in the afternoon.

"I, ah, made cookies today," Ellie said, nodding at the plate in her hand to prove it. "I...I thought the children might like some."

"Chocolate chip?" Georgie asked hopefully.

Ellie laughed. "Mmm-hmm."

"Yum. I'll get ever'body," and he took off at a run.

"Come in," Nona invited, but Ellie no sooner stepped through the door than she was surrounded by children.

Taking the plate of cookies from her, Nona laughed. "Here, Laila," she said, handing the plate to one of the older girls. "Take these to the kitchen and share them, please. Miss Ellie and I are going into the back garden."

Thank goodness, Ellie thought with an inward sigh of relief. The back garden was exactly where she wanted to go.

Without even a hint, Nona led her to the tiki, or whatever it was, still holding court among the hibiscus bushes near the back fence.

The carved image scowled back at them as usual, but today it seemed exactly that, Ellie thought. Just a carved image.

But it was she who assumed Daniel was in the carving. Daniel himself thought he was in a tree.

Turning her attention to the tree growing in the garden behind the hibiscus bushes, Ellie studied it, her gaze wandering up its trunk and searching among its leafy branches.

She had no idea what kind of tree it was, but nothing about it indicated it was more than it was, either.

Her gaze dropped again to the tiki. In the light breeze, a hibiscus blossom brushed against its frowning countenance.

When its scowl never wavered, Ellie gave a small disappointed half laugh. The thing wasn't ticklish. Carved deep within the scowl, the caverns representing its eyes seemed empty.

Nobody home, Ellie thought in defeat.

"Are you all right, dear?" Nona asked.

Silently Ellie nodded. She was all right. It was Daniel who was somewhere horrible. And she didn't know where to find him.

With Daniel gone, Ellie and Chad ordered pizza in, topping it off with Ellie's apple pie, which neither of them particularly wanted.

Daniel's disappearance made even Chad unusually quiet. Finally Ellie put her fork down and sighed.

"You know Daniel disappears, don't you?"

"I know," he replied, and washed down the last of his pie with a big glass of milk.

"No, I mean *literally* disappears."

He looked at her. "I *know,* El."

"But why?" Ellie asked in frustration. "Why is he here one minute and gone the next? What makes him go and come like that?"

Without waiting for Chad's answer, she continued. "He almost disappeared earlier today," she told her brother. "Chad, I could see through him. I really could. But he became solid again almost at once, so I thought the episode was over. We puttered around here all afternoon, and he looked as normal and healthy as you. There was no indication at all that…that what happened this morning would happen again. There were no *symptoms.*"

"Not everything is a medical problem, Ellie," Chad reminded her gently.

"I know."

"And you know I deploy out of here in a few days."

She knew that, too, Ellie thought. Her plane ticket was for the evening before Chad's departure date.

Representing the family as she did, all of whom missed her brother as much as he missed them, she'd planned it that way deliberately so she could be with Chad as long as possible before he left for Japan.

"Two more days," Ellie said, and rose to take their dishes to the sink.

Chad, however, shooed her away. "I'll get these. Go put your feet up."

But Ellie chose to stand beside him and rinse as he washed up their few dishes.

Much as she and Daniel had done that afternoon, she thought. Only then the two of them stood close enough for their shoulders to brush.

"It's not fair," she suddenly said fiercely. "Daniel is a good man. He doesn't deserve this."

And neither do I, she wanted to cry out to the *whatever* holding Daniel prisoner and now seemed to hold her prisoner, too.

Though Ellie went to bed early, the clock on the nightstand said midnight and she still lay wakeful, her mind on constant replay of the day's events.

They ended, as always, in the Kamehanas' back garden, where Daniel said he was, yet where the tiki was just a carving, the trees and flowers no more than the natural flora they were, and with no sight of Daniel, or the essence of Daniel, anywhere.

Scrunching the pillow under her neck, Ellie pictured the tiki yet again. Its scowl, its fierce grimace, its shadowed eyes. All carved into a block of wood, an artist's imagining, their reality a result of the artist's talent. Interesting, but certainly without soul.

She hadn't thought so the first time she'd seen the carving, though. Then, she'd thought the thing winked at her. And later she thought it had the loneliest eyes she'd ever seen.

Imagination, she supposed. With its features partly obscured by the many plumeria leis hanging around its close-to-nonexistent neck, the colored party lights and night shadows cast by moonlight gave the thing a semblance of expression.

But the next time she saw the carving, Ellie thought sleepily, sinking deeper into the pillow, she was with Nona and it was broad daylight. She'd thought the carving looked sad then, too, though its scowl was breathtakingly ugly.

Nona, she remembered, reached out and caressed its cheek. Plumeria blossoms lay scattered on the earth in front of it.

There were no plumeria blossoms today....

Ellie's eyes widened in the darkness. There were no plumeria blossoms today!

Daniel said that he could only communicate when

Nona brought plumerias to him. Was that why the garden seemed so empty? So lifeless?

She sat up on an elbow.

Of course it was. She had no sense of Daniel in the garden because he had no way to reach out!

But another thought sent her back against the pillow with a sigh of defeat. Even when she could sense Daniel's presence in the tiki, she'd couldn't communicate with him as Nona did.

And even had she been up to her ears in plumerias this afternoon, she couldn't release him from the tiki.

But he was *there*. She knew it!

So what did make him physically appear to her? *Phhtt,* he was there...she smiled in the darkness and swallowed against the lump in her throat...and *phhtt,* he was gone.

There were no plumerias about when she'd first seen him at the beach, she thought sleepily. Except her silver earrings.

Nor were any of the exotic blossoms present at Chad's barbecue when she'd seen Daniel again. The women at the party were dressed as casually as the men that night, their only flowers possibly on someone's printed fabric, though Ellie didn't remember seeing even that.

She'd been wearing Gram's earrings again, but they hardly counted.

Plumeria, the Flower of Hawaii. Made Especially for You by Ohana.

Ellie wondered where Gram bought them. Was *Ohana* the name of the department store?

But *ohana* meant family. Such a lovely word for what Daniel didn't have. Not what Ellie considered family, anyway.

Family rejoiced because you were alive. They didn't berate you for not coming back sooner so you could marry some stupid girl with connections.

Ohana meant far more than that! From their cradles, Gram taught the Simmses that family meant you loved and cared for each other, especially in bad times or when circumstances were beyond your control.

The flower of Hawaii, she thought muzzily. *Made especially for you by Ohana.* Lovely.

On a long slow sigh, she finally drifted into…

Ellie sat straight up, her eyes wide-open and unbelieving.

"Gram!" she breathed, the soft exclamation escalating into an outraged howl.

"Darn you, Grammie," she yelled. "What the heck have you done?"

Chapter Ten

"Ellie!" Gram said sleepily. "Is everything all right, dear?"

Chad appeared in Ellie's doorway looking disheveled and more than ready to do somebody major harm.

"Go away," Ellie told him coldly. "You knew about this, you traitor. I'll deal with you later."

She returned her attention to the cell phone at her ear. "Funny you should ask that, Gram," she said sweetly, watching Chad slink away. "I thought you might want to know the earrings you gave me have been the highlight of my vacation."

Her irony went right over her grandmother's head. "I'm sure they're lovely, darling, and I'm glad you're enjoying them, but it's four in the morning here."

"Really? It's midnight in the tropics," Ellie replied sweetly. "And I want to talk about my earrings *now*."

"Watch your tone, Eliza Ann. What about them?"

"You lied to me, for one thing. When I asked, you told me you bought them."

"No, I didn't. I told you I got them in a little out-of-the-way place when I visited the islands years ago. I never said I *bought* them. Actually, they were given to me by a distant cousin."

"All right, you didn't actually say it. But you knew I thought that's what you meant."

"Which goes to show that sometimes you think too much, Ellie," her grandmother replied gently. "You must follow your heart. It's a lot more reliable."

Ellie sighed. It was hard to stay mad at her grandmother for long. "What was your cousin's name, Gram?" she asked at last.

"Rachel, dear."

"Rachel what?"

"Rachel Kamehana. Do you know her?"

Why was she not surprised? "Everyone here calls her Nona," Ellie replied evenly. "And she lives next door to Chad. You knew that, I imagine."

"Why, no! What a wonderful coincidence."

Wasn't it just.

"Still, the Great Ones never deal with coincidence," her grandmother added slowly, "so it was bound to happen."

"Bound to," Ellie echoed.

She heard her grandmother sigh. "Ellie, darling, what *is* wrong? Aren't you having a good time? Chad said you'd met someone."

The weasel.

"Oh, I've met someone, all right. When I wear your

earrings, he follows me around like a puppy, and when I take them off, he disappears into a block of wood. I'm having the time of my life, thanks to your little giftie."

There was silence on the other end. Finally Gram replied, her voice uncharacteristically tentative. "Don't you like him, Ellie?"

Closing her eyes, Ellie pressed the phone to her ear and bowed her head, wishing she was in her grandmother's arms right now. Or Daniel's.

"Yes," she whispered. "I like him, Gram. And I think he likes me, too. But it's a dead-end situation. For him, and for me."

"Tell me," Gram said, and all the love in the world reached out through her voice to wrap Ellie in its arms.

Leaning back into her pillow, Ellie told her grandmother everything.

"So you see, even if I wore the earrings forever there's no way of untangling ourselves from this mess," she concluded.

"Of course there is, darling. And you will find it. The Great Ones never send a gift without love in it for you. Somewhere in your heart, and in Daniel's heart, and in those earrings, there's a way to set Daniel free so you can both get on with your lives."

"Do you really think so?"

"I know so."

"Then I hope so," Ellie replied. "But you do know that whether he is free or not, Daniel and I will never be an item."

"Never is a long time, Ellie."

"Yes, it is. And Daniel has a—a fiancée to marry and I have a career. I promised LeAnne."

"A career and a husband are not mutually exclusive, darling. Many women juggle both quite easily."

"Juggle is right. And it's the woman's career that gets shortchanged. I'm a pediatric nurse, Gram, and that's all I want to be. Not someone's wife, not someone's girlfriend or significant other. Men, I've found, say they're willing to share, but they seldom are."

"That's a rather sweeping statement, Eliza Ann."

"Perhaps. But I'm not willing to chance being wrong."

"I worry about you, darling."

"I know. All of you do. The family just has to understand that not every woman is cut out to be a wife and mother. After all, someone has to be a doting aunt to the nieces and nephews," Ellie replied, trying to lighten the conversation before she started crying in earnest.

Her grandmother gave in and allowed her the last word. "If you say so, Ellie. Now, wear those pretty earrings and enjoy your Daniel while you can. At least you have that. Good night, darling."

"Good night, Gram," Ellie replied softly. "And thanks." She held the phone to her breast a moment before placing it on the nightstand.

The earrings, she thought. And Chad had known. That's why he encouraged her to wear them all the time.

Reaching over, she turned off the lamp beside the bed. She'd deal with her little brother in the morning.

Sinking into her pillow once more, she drew in an exhausted breath...only to whoosh it out again.

The earrings!

In seconds, Ellie had a pair of sweatpants pulled on under the oversize T-shirt she wore to sleep in, and was frantically poking the silver plumerias into her ears as she ran to the patio door.

Sure enough, a shadowy form stood near the picnic table where she'd found him several times before—the outer perimeter of the earrings' reach, she now realized.

But what on earth was Daniel doing, jiggling and twitching like that?

As she approached, however, she saw he was in the act of pulling a T-shirt over his head—what he must have been doing in the bathroom earlier when she'd taken the earrings off.

His head popped through the neck, his face wearing a look of total confusion.

"Criminy!" he said, borrowing her favorite expression.

Ellie laughed. "I'll bet you were doing that when you left."

He looked blank a moment. "Guess I was. For a second I didn't know what the hell was going on."

"I'm sorry," Ellie said, sobering immediately. "It was my fault."

Daniel wrapped his arms around her. "C'mon, El. You can't take the blame for this. Something's playing with me. That's all."

"But it *is* my fault!" Ellie exclaimed, looking up at him. "It's my earrings. When I wear them, you—you're here. And when I take them off, you go back to the Kamehanas'."

He considered it, but finally shook his head. "I don't think so. I know you mean well, honey, but earrings and the *whatever* in the cove don't, uh, have much in common."

"Not just any earrings," Ellie said impatiently. How like a man to need every *i* dotted.

Grabbing Daniel's hand, she pulled him across the lawn and into Chad's apartment. The living room had no overhead light, but she turned on the lamp beside the couch.

"*These* earrings!" she said, shoving back her hair.

He smiled, touched one, and pulled Ellie close.

"Pretty," he said. "And pretty on you. I mean it. But you see a lot of this kind of thing here. Don't take this wrong, El, but you can buy flower jewelry like this everywhere in the islands. Besides, *earrings?* A shell necklace maybe, or a special piece of volcanic stone."

Ellie rolled her eyes. "That is *sooo* hackneyed. Daniel, the Great Ones never do things according to the storybooks. *Look* at them!" With her fingers behind her ears, she thrust their lobes forward.

He looked. And looked again. And paled visibly.

"Plumerias," he said flatly.

"Plumerias. And my gram gave them to me. Remember I told you about Gram's little gifts? I thought she'd bought them. I called her tonight and it turns out Nona gave them to her."

"You mean Nona had the way of setting me free and she gave it away?"

His face wore a look of such hurt surprise that Ellie couldn't stand it. Standing on tiptoe, she quickly kissed his cheek.

"It's been at least twenty years since my grandmother came to Hawaii, Daniel. You were a little boy then. Unless Nona can read the future, she couldn't have known what the earrings would do. My grandmother didn't and was surprised when I told her. Gram just knows when things are...special. Then, when the Great Ones tell her, she gives that specialness away."

Or when she thinks one of the family needs it, Ellie thought. But that part she kept to herself.

"If I didn't live in a tree, I'd think you were an ounce short of a full quart," Daniel said slowly. "As it is, I'll buy it if you do."

By this time they were sitting on the couch with Ellie tucked up under Daniel's arm. His hand, hanging over her shoulder, held one of hers.

At his comment, however, she glanced up at him. "You, um, don't live in a tree. You live in a wood carving."

"What!"

"A mud-ugly tiki," she elaborated, beginning to enjoy this. "But Nona doesn't think it's an actual representation of a god, just similar. You know, fat flat nose, lots of big teeth in a wide snarling mouth, long head bigger than the body. And did I mention ugly?"

He laughed. "You're in love, I can tell."

Ellie froze...and knew when he went as still as she that Daniel's words caught him by surprise, too.

"You might say that," she acknowledged softly. How long had she known? From the cradle perhaps, but only realized it a second ago.

Daniel's hand gripped hers tightly.

"You might say that about me, too," he said.

On top of her head, Ellie felt the light pressure of his lips against her hair, but he didn't turn her around.

Grateful for that, Ellie kissed the hand near her face still holding her own.

But she had to say it. "It doesn't mean anything, though, because it's not going anywhere."

"It means everything," Daniel countered. "But you're right. It's not going anywhere."

"I'm leaving in two days," she whispered miserably. She had to say that, too. "My vacation is over and I have a job to return to. Want to return to."

Ellie closed her eyes, glad that Daniel couldn't see her face, and equally glad she couldn't see his.

Behind her she felt the stretch of his body as he reached for the lamp and plunged the room into darkness. His arm then came around to pull her closer into his chest.

Outside the uncurtained patio doors across the room, the moon did its best against the darkness.

A cricket chirped monotonously.

All safe, Ellie thought sadly, wrapped in Daniel's arms. Crickets grow silent when there is danger.

The back of her head rested against Daniel's broad chest, but even so, she felt the low steady thrum of his heart. Across the way, the kitchen clock counted the seconds, its faint tick, tick, tick punctuating the quiet.

Two days.

When Ellie awoke, she lay on the couch under a light blanket with her head propped on one of the hard sofa pillows.

She sat up, rubbing the ear she'd been sleeping on. Her lobe felt hot and sore.

Daniel and Chad were just beyond in the kitchen

area, each of them holding a coffee cup. When she stood, they turned and looked at her.

"Good morning," Chad greeted, far too cheerily. With uncharacteristic brotherly generosity, he handed her a cup of coffee.

Giving him time to stew, Ellie blew on it, sipped, then leveled her cold stare at him. *"Traitor."*

"C'mon, El. Be fair. You know none of us interferes when Gram gives a gift. Besides, I didn't know right away, either. Not until you took the earrings off in the car when we were coming home from the club and suddenly I didn't have a back seat passenger anymore."

"Huh!" She took another sip of the delicious coffee. Chad couldn't cook, but he made a cup of coffee to die for.

She'd avoided looking at Daniel, not knowing quite what to say to him after what was said and what wasn't said the night before. Aware that she looked grubby and disheveled, she glanced at him now.

And found him looking back at her as if she were the delicious coffee she held so tenderly in her hands.

"I was just telling Dan here," Chad said, "that I have to go in to work today. Damn shame, too, because I..."

For the first time Ellie noticed her brother wore his cammies.

"No!" she wailed, huffiness forgotten. "Darn it, Chad, you're supposed to be off today. Tell them you can't come in. We were going do something special today. You said you had something planned."

"Sorry, El. The marines giveth days off and they taketh them away. Blessed be their name." He laughed. "Blessings aren't usually what they get, though. But I have two tickets for a whale-watching trip that I'll lose if you and Dan don't use them."

"Oh, Chad."

"Look, man, are you sure?" Daniel said. "Why don't you call in sick? I'm a doctor. I'll sign your note or whatever."

"And I'm a marine, bud," Chad replied dryly. "We don't do notes."

He gave Daniel one of those man-to-man looks that excluded Ellie completely.

"You're doing me a favor," he added. "I was feeling bad about leaving El on her own again. But with you here, I know she won't be lonesome."

"That's a bit thick, brother, even for you," Ellie said, beginning to get suspicious.

Chad grinned at her. "I'm hitching a ride in with a friend of mine, so use my car. It's a lunch cruise, by the way, and you should be there an hour ahead. Keys, tickets and directions are on the counter."

With a quick buss on Ellie's cheek, he was gone.

"Looks like we're watching whales today," Daniel commented.

"Looks like."

Their gazes caught.

Busy, Ellie thought. They should stay very busy.

When Chad finally saw his car pull out of the drive, he made his goodbyes and went back downstairs to his own apartment.

It was his day off, and he damned sure wasn't spending it in cammies.

* * *

They saw spouts in the distance, and from very far away they saw a fluke, but for the most part the whales chose to ignore the tourists.

It didn't matter.

The tables were close in the dining room, the lines to the buffet long and three deep, yet the only conversation Ellie heard was Daniel's. On deck, they stood shoulder to shoulder with dozens of others at the rail searching the horizon for the whales they'd all come to see, but the only contact Daniel felt was Ellie's.

They, too, scanned the horizon, as excited as the others by a distant sighting, as delighted as the rest when a pair of dolphins decided to body surf the wake of the ship for a while. But Ellie's true excitement was in the way the wind ruffled Daniel's hair, and Daniel's true delight was in Ellie's laughter.

When they left the ship, it was still early afternoon. Knowing she was leaving soon…one day, nine hours and twenty-five minutes…Ellie needed to do some shopping.

So they wandered the shops for a while, Daniel buying a few articles of clothing and Ellie picking up gifts for various small cousins and her sister, Marlie's, young ones, for whom she was such a good aunt.

And back at the apartment, Chad was there to greet them, once more a welcome third; someone to dilute the closeness she and Daniel wanted so much yet didn't want at all.

To help Chad clean out his groceries and because she wanted to give her brother a last home-cooked meal—

and Daniel, too, she thought—Ellie prepared a Texas Sunday dinner that night.

Fried chicken, mashed potatoes and gravy, cooked carrots, steamed broccoli, a green salad and iced tea—with the last of the apple pie she'd made the day before.

After the past couple of years of microwave dinners, it tasted pretty good to her, too, Ellie thought, watching the two men so dear to her chow down. Cooking was the one thing she missed about not being married. It just wasn't the same without an appreciative eater to cook for.

Unlike her ex-husband, however, these two men insisted on doing the dishes, and this time there wasn't enough room in the kitchen area for her to join them. So she sat on the couch and watched a television program she neither saw nor heard until they joined her, bringing mugs of coffee to finish off the evening.

"What are you going to do about the earrings, El?" her brother asked when she switched off the TV.

Trust Chad to get to the heart of the matter in the shortest possible time, Ellie thought.

Heart of the matter. Her sister, Marlie the punster, would love that one.

Ellie sighed. "I don't know. I've thought about it all day, but everything I come up with seems risky. Or heartless."

She could make a pun, too, it seemed. "If I keep the earrings and go back to Texas, Daniel is trapped until I return."

Daniel sat in a chair opposite hers, but when he half smiled, the old familiar something zinged between them. Ellie forgot what she was talking about.

"Um, what I mean is, I can't give Daniel the earrings because he disappears too fast when I remove them."

Reaching up, she rubbed a sore lobe. She'd been wearing the earrings all day and much of the night before.

"And even if I could, or if he personally removes them from my ears, what if he gets zapped back to the tiki anyway? We'd have no way of getting him out again."

And trust Chad to come up with just the right suggestion. "Ask Nona," he said.

Before Ellie could reply, Daniel stood. "You're right. We'll do it. But we'll do it tomorrow. Tonight Ellie is tired and the earrings are hurting her. I need to go."

"No!" Ellie leaped to her feet and grabbed his arm, as if he would disappear right then and there.

"No, Daniel," she repeated. "I don't want you going back to that thing ever again. The earrings don't bother me. Really. I'll put alcohol on my ears and they'll be fine. You'll sleep here tonight."

When her brother raised an eyebrow, she scowled at him. "On the couch," she said evenly. Though if it were her apartment, the sleeping arrangements would be altogether different.

Chad gave her his best innocent-brother look. "I didn't say a word."

But Daniel took Ellie's hand.

"You'll excuse us," he told Chad formally. Without waiting for a reply he led her through the patio doors and into the night.

"Sure," Chad called after them. "Don't mind me!"

Once away from the apartment lights, Daniel took

Ellie in his arms. He didn't kiss her mouth; instead he lightly kissed her ears. Each one.

Oh, Ellie thought dreamily. The man certainly had the gift of touch. His fingers, his mouth, his tongue turned every place they contacted to warm butter, to slow-moving molten lava.

And every place he didn't touch silently begged and pleaded for his attention.

"Take them off, Ellie," he whispered, breathing the words against her ear.

For answer, she turned her face and captured his traitorous mouth with her own. Did this magic man think she was crazy? She knew a good thing when it kissed her, and she wasn't ever letting it go.

Not until tomorrow night, at least.

But the wisp of thought was all it took to pull her out of the spell Daniel's hands and mouth wove so easily over her body.

"Take them off, Ellie," he repeated softly. "Heaven knows we can't go any farther, though surely heaven knows how much I want to."

He kissed each of her closed eyes. Behind her lids she felt the warmth of his lips, and heard the medical practicality in his advice.

"Your ears hurt," he said. "And they're too warm to the touch. I've been where I've been for years and one more night won't hurt me. Go inside now, take these pretty things out, swab your lobes with alcohol and rub some ointment on them."

With his palm cupping her neck, he touched a lobe gently with his thumb. The low-level pain was immediate. He was right. If she didn't take the earrings out soon, she was asking for infection.

"But I don't want to," she whispered miserably.

He stepped away from her. "Do it anyway," he said. "Tomorrow you'll wear the earrings all day, until you leave for your plane or until we get Nona's advice. But tonight I have something you can wear in their place."

Reaching into his pocket, he pulled out a small box.

When Ellie opened it, starlight gleamed on silver. A tiny leaping dolphin hung from a silver chain.

"Ohhh," she whispered, touching it with one finger.

Taking it from the box, Daniel fastened it around her neck, then wrapped her in his arms. "It's not magic like your earrings," he said quietly, "but I hope it reminds you that some things are simply magical unto themselves, like this day has been."

Tucked up next to him, Ellie listened to Daniel's heart beat steadily beneath her ear for a moment. Then deliberately she crossed the unspoken line they'd both avoided.

"What will you do if Nona can use the earrings to free you?"

Daniel didn't answer right away. "Go home," he said at last. "Find out why Laura waited. Do what I must." He sighed softly. "But right now, it's time for you to go. We'll talk tomorrow. Be sure you take off the earrings. I want to know you're resting when I think of you tonight."

Turning her gently, he aimed her toward the apartment. "Sleep well."

* * *

Surprisingly, Ellie did sleep well—deep and dreamlessly. In the morning, before she even had a first cup of coffee, she put on the earrings.

In seconds Daniel walked through the door, and they had their coffee together.

It would be so easy to get used to the simple pleasure of this, Ellie thought as the two of them sat at Chad's small table without speaking.

If, that is, she didn't have a life and a career so intertwined there was nothing left of her to share.

Or if Daniel, who didn't take honor lightly, didn't have a fiancée who waited for him.

Whatever happened with the earrings, both she and Daniel were as bound by circumstance as they'd ever been. In truth, neither of them was free.

But they had today.

They watched television. Morning-edition news, game shows, talk shows.

They washed clothes. Dried them. Folded them.

They talked. Of Ellie's wish to someday join IMO, the International Medical Organization. Of Daniel's wish to practice medicine among those who needed him, now that he understood the nature of his calling.

They laughed. At the wrenching dramas on daytime soaps. At Chad's valentine-printed boxers.

They commiserated. Daniel with Ellie's homesickness. Ellie with Daniel's dread of returning home at all.

And they danced. Apart, to the upbeat music on a variety of radio stations. Together, to the dreamy music of an oldies station. Daniel, an authority after years of watching little girls practice in the Kamehanas' back garden, even taught Ellie the rudiments of the hula.

They didn't speak of love. And they didn't speak of alternatives.

Ellie packed while Daniel watched silently. He folded his few pieces of clothing and placed them in the chest of drawers in the bedroom she was using. She didn't comment, either.

Through the day Chad was in and out. He had his own packing to do, errands to run, military details to take care of. He introduced them to the marine taking over the apartment, explaining to the man that Daniel kept clothing there but without going into the circumstances.

It was possible of course, that Daniel would never need those clothes, but none of them went into that, either.

To clean out the refrigerator, Ellie prepared leftovers for lunch. And when the kitchen was clean and there was nothing else to put away, fold or pack, she and Daniel walked hand in hand next door.

Nona answered their knock.

"This is Daniel Morgan," Ellie said, wondering if the old woman would have recognized him without the introduction. "Daniel, this is Rachel Kamehana."

"Nona," the old woman corrected and laughed. "You've talked to your grandmother, I see."

She tilted her head and looked Daniel up and down, her eyes bright and mischievous. "And you came to see my lawn ornament."

Her statement caught both of them off guard, but

Daniel recovered first. "Yes, if you don't mind. Ellie, uh, told me about it."

Nona chuckled. "I can imagine. Come along." And she opened the door for them to follow her through the house and into the back garden.

Beneath the lush hibiscus bushes, the tiki scowled out at the world with vacant, shadowed eyes and a wooden snarl. Just wood, Ellie thought. The thing exhibited no personality when Daniel wasn't in it.

But Daniel stared at his erstwhile home in shock, and Ellie felt a faint trembling in the hand he'd kept wrapped around hers most of the day.

"I think he's rather handsome," Nona said, tilting her head as she, too, examined the carving, "but some days he's more handsome than others."

It was all the opening Ellie needed. "Did you know my earrings would release Daniel?" she asked, doing her best not to sound accusing.

"I've always known the earrings were special," Nona replied quietly, "but I never knew in what way. My grandmother gave them to me and told me to follow my heart in what I chose to do with them."

She smiled. "I chose to give them to your grandmother when she came here. And she chose to give them to you. What will you choose to do with them?"

"Whatever it takes to keep Daniel free," Ellie answered at once. "But I don't know what that is. We're hoping you can help us."

"I doubt it," Nona said slowly. "But tell me how the earrings work."

"When I wear them, Daniel comes to me, but only

to me. When I take them off, he gets zapped back into that thing. Nona, I can't wear them forever," Ellie said, fighting tears again. "I have my life as a nurse, and Daniel has a practice and a—a fiancée waiting for him."

The words almost choked her, there was something so very wrong with them. Yet she spoke the absolute truth.

The truth should set her free, right?

She felt the soft squeeze of Daniel's hand.

"And if Daniel removes them himself?" Nona asked.

Daniel frowned at the tiki, squatting among the flowers. "We've thought of that," he said. "But if I'm pulled back inside this fellow, anyway, then Ellie has lost her earrings and I'm back where I started, this time with no bit of magic to get me out again."

Merely the thought caused Ellie's throat to squeeze shut, and she turned her face into Daniel's chest.

"What should we do?" she heard him ask Nona quietly.

Taking a deep breath, for courage and for the sheer pleasure of this man's scent, Ellie too faced the old woman.

"I don't know," Nona replied. "You see, I only knew the earrings were connected to this—" she gave the tiki a gentle pat "—when I saw Ellie's fascination with it." She rubbed a gentle hand over the carved head, then looked at Daniel for a long moment. "I don't think the Old Ones are sure what they want to do," she told him.

"But I know this. Whatever connection the earrings have with your freedom, they only work on this island, and they only work with you and Ellie. A pair for a pair, you see. No matter what the two of you choose to do with them, unless the Old Ones are a third party in the agreement, you will remain here, Daniel. Plumerias, my dears, even silver ones, are the flower of Hawaii."

Again, the old woman rubbed her hand over the wooden head of the tiki. "Still," she said slowly, "it's possible what you and Eliza Ann have is larger than the earrings, though I don't know. You hold Ellie's hand, but speak of a different woman, and Ellie holds yours and speaks of distance."

Her voice turned brisk. "Do as you will with the earrings, since they seem the only true connection you have. Perhaps the Old Ones will set you free, Daniel. Or perhaps they will not."

Chapter Eleven

On the tiny haunted beach where they'd first met, Ellie and Daniel stood before a silvered highway leading across the sea to a low-riding moon. In only a couple of hours, however, Ellie would fly over it.

Each of them wore the lei of scarlet plumerias Nona gave them earlier that afternoon. Ellie fought the urge to rip hers from her neck and throw it away.

Its scent would forever remind her of Daniel, she thought, and what they'd had. And couldn't have.

There were no words for tonight's goodbye. Too much was at stake.

Daniel had decided to remove Ellie's earrings—if he could. Yet no matter what happened as a result, they knew that tonight ended an enchantment having nothing to do with a pair of silver flowers.

If he were freed, Daniel had obligations to his family and to a loyal fiancée. If he was not...well, that didn't bear talking about.

Either way, Ellie's future lay only in the profession she'd dedicated to her lost child.

A light breeze caressed Ellie's face and brushed against the lei about her neck so that its petals tickled her throat. The necklace of flowers seemed to choke her.

She shivered and turned to Daniel.

"Well..." she began, only to have his long-fingered doctor's hands cup her face and tilt it toward him. The play of moonlight over his features silenced her.

"I love you, Ellie," he said huskily, saying the actual words for the first time. "I always will."

When Ellie bowed her head, her mouth tilted into the valley of his cupped hands. "I love you, too," she whispered, and knew that Daniel's palms caught her tears.

She looked up at him then. "I'm so sorry."

"Hush."

It hurt too much to linger.

Using both hands to brush her hair back over her shoulders, Daniel unhooked an earring.

Each of them held their breath.

A jolt pummeled Daniel's body and his pulse raced for a moment, then slowed and steadied. He felt nauseous and insubstantial.

With the earring now in his fist, he looked into Ellie's frightened but determined face. Her small hands held each of his larger ones in a death grip.

For such a dainty woman, his Ellie was a fighter through and through. But he wasn't.

God help him, when it came right down to it, he couldn't take the chance of living out the rest of his life in a carved wooden log.

"See if you can walk away from me, Ellie," he said gruffly.

Her eyes widened, but almost immediately she understood.

Turning away, she walked slowly toward the street that ran through the neighborhood behind them.

Daniel watched her go, feeling his heart being snatched from his chest.

But then Ellie came running back to him, her pale hair streaming behind. When he caught her in his arms, she laughed. "You're free, Daniel! You're free!"

She raised her face, and he kissed each of her shining eyes. "Now you take out the other," he said

Ellie looked stricken. "Daniel, no. You do it."

He shook his head. "I'm still here, El, but something isn't right. I feel it in my gut, literally. Do you know what I mean?"

At her nod, he added, "I want to see if I can remain without you wearing the earring. This way, if I wind up back in the Kamehanas' garden you can get me out again, and we can try something else."

Never taking her eyes from his face, Ellie slowly removed the other earring.

A thud echoed through Daniel's already queasy belly, but he remained on the beach. He let out the breath he hadn't realized he held.

But when Ellie held the silver flower out to him, he shook his head.

"Can't do it," he told her matter-of-factly. "Don't ask me how I know, but your earrings have done all they can do. If I take them both, I'll be the Kamehanas' lawn ornament for the rest of my life. As it is, I think I'm probably stuck on this part of the island, but I suppose there are worse places."

He smiled, wishing Ellie would smile back at him. Instead, her sweet face looked the way he felt.

His Ellie didn't stay down long, however. Within seconds bereft turned to grimly determined.

"I'll be back," she said fiercely, "on my very next vacation. Then I'm wearing both my earrings and we're going *dancing!*"

But she put up a hand and cupped his cheek. "Will you be all right until then?" she asked. "I'll have Chad tell his buddy you'll be sharing the apartment."

"Or I'll talk to Nona," Daniel replied. He hadn't thought through the logistics of the thing but with his debit card and Nona's help, he had no doubt he could manage something.

He hugged Ellie to him.

And this woman made of moonlight would be back. He could live on that thought forever, if he had to.

"Chad told me," Ellie said, her voice wobbly but determined, "if a visitor to the islands throws her lei into the ocean and it floats back to shore, it's a sign she'll return."

Lifting the lei from around her neck, she threw it as far as she could over the water before them. It landed on the surface in a perfect silver-gilt circle, floating there gently.

They watched it for a minute, but it didn't seem to move.

No Ellie, no Daniel, Daniel thought. Removing his lei, he too cast it over the water.

It landed with one edge of its own perfect circle draping over Ellie's, making Daniel think of entwined rings on a wedding invitation.

He felt such a yearning surge through him that for a moment he forgot his belly-roiling nausea.

The twined circlets of flowers undulated on top of the water, silver shadows atop silvery moonlight, tantalizing them with their bob and sway.

Hand in hand Daniel and Ellie watched...and realized the swaying bobbing leis were actually edging toward shore.

Ellie laughed and turned her smiling face toward Daniel—the look Daniel had waited for all night.

"Aloha, Ellie," he whispered, and kissed her one last time.

A faint honk from the street—Chad, coming to take her to the airport—and she was gone.

Daniel watched the glow of headlights as Chad made a U-turn and disappeared. Not wanting company, he'd long since decided to spend the night at the cove. Time enough tomorrow to ask Nona about how to handle his new situation.

After the embrace the old woman gave him earlier in the day when he and Ellie left her house, he had no doubt Nona would help him. And she'd told him to come to her, assuring him he was more than a cousin.

Ellie had her Grammie; now Daniel had Nona. Not quite the same, perhaps, but close enough.

Turning away from the dark neighborhood behind, Daniel again faced the sea—and found the leis had separated on the water. Instead of overlapping, they now floated side by side.

Ah, well. Enough of signs and portents. Such thinking could drive a man crazy. That the leis had entwined at all was merely an accident of the toss.

Finding a comfortable spot, he lowered himself to the sand just beyond the water's edge. He missed Ellie already, even though for the first time in years he found himself both free of the tiki and with some privacy. Truth was, he'd enjoyed being Ellie's shadow for a while.

Raising the silver earring to his lips, he kissed it, his gaze automatically searching the river of light before him for their leis.

One of them, a few feet from the shoreline now, floated gently forward. The other…

Where was the other?

Daniel stood again, the better to scan the shoreline, the beach, the ocean as far out as he could see in the bright moonlight. But all he found, all he could locate, was the one sodden lei, now lying among the shells and lacy froth left behind on the beach.

The sea had kept the other.

But whose had it kept? His…or Ellie's?

His, probably. After all, the tradition of tossing the lei into the sea was in hopes of returning. Since one had to leave in order to return, well, *he* wasn't going anywhere.

So it was Ellie's lei lying in the sand.

Wasn't it?

It was. She'd promised to return, and she would.

He dropped to the sand near the wet and bedraggled circlet of flowers but didn't pick it up. Ellie's lei belonged to the cove now. When she came back, he would have another one for her.

Idly, he lifted his head to gaze at a sky full of stars trying to make a show against the light of the moon.

It wasn't the stars that held his attention, however, but the occasional lights that arced toward the horizon with a distinctive powerful hum. This area of sky was part of the flight path used by Hawaii's air traffic.

In about half an hour, Daniel estimated, he would see Ellie's plane carrying her back to Texas. Would he know which light it was?

In answer, his nerve endings zinged toward the curls and angles of the silver flower nestled protectively in his palm.

He'd know.

The earring in his hand was far more than his key to freedom; it was his connection to Ellie. His comfort. His knowledge that for the first time in his life, he truly loved and was loved in return.

Though he still felt nauseous and shaky, knowing Ellie was a part of his life as long as he had the earring was a gift beyond price.

He thought of her. Her wonderful heart-stopping smile. Her moonlight hair. Her gift for empathetic practicality. He could easily spend the rest of his life sitting on this beach dreaming of Ellie.

That is, the part of his life when Ellie wasn't actually here. When she came back, they were going dancing.

Picturing himself dancing with Ellie, Daniel smiled into the night.

Except for the ever-present murmur of the sea and an occasional night bird, it was whisper quiet. Each muted drone of the infrequent air traffic high above could be heard distinctly.

Now she would be boarding, he thought. Filing onto the plane and looking for her seat. He doubted the practical Ellie Simms flew first class.

Now she was placing her carry-on in the overhead bin, settling into her seat. A window seat? Would she look out into the night as the plane took off, her eyes straining to see this tiny cove in the darkness?

Now the plane taxied down the runway. Now lifted over the Pacific.

There, Daniel thought. That was it. He stood, his gaze following a blinking light moving steadily over the water toward the moon, carrying with it all his hopeless dreams.

Carrying with it all his heart.

A low distant roar melded with the powerful whisper of the sea, and he knew it for the sound of his own despair.

A sputter.

His head lifted sharply.

Put-a, put-put-put-put.

No! It couldn't be!

The distant light, its red light blinking, looked as though it stood still in the sky.

One lei, the other taken. One silver plumeria where there should be two.

"Noooooooo!"

Without thought, Daniel splashed forward into the sea, his feet kicking up cascades of silver.

"You have *me!*" he bellowed as he ran ever deeper. "You can't have her, too!"

When depth forced him to slow, he drew back his arm and flung the earring as far as he could in front of him. "Take it, damn you. It's yours. Leave Ellie alone. Take *me!*" And he dove.

The water grabbed him immediately, pulling him down, down into its black liquid nothingness. *Me!* His mind continued to scream. *Not Ellie! Take me! I'm the fool! Not her! Never her!*

Until he thought no more. Felt no more. Was no more.

Ellie knew, as soon as the plane lifted off and she peered out the window beside her, straining for a last glimpse of the cove somewhere among the twinkling lights of O'ahu, that she was going home, resigning her job effective immediately and returning on the next available plane.

To heck with waiting for a vacation that wouldn't come for at least another few months. Hawaii teemed with children, and a good nurse could find a job anywhere.

No way was she leaving Daniel alone in the Kamehanas' garden locked in a tiki that wasn't even a tiki. If she had to, she'd throw the thing in the fire herself.

Hmmm. She and Daniel should have thought of that.

Yet they hadn't thought of much at all but each other and what *wasn't* going to work—she an always-on-call nurse and he with a waiting fiancée and family obligations.

The lights of the island disappeared, leaving nothing but moon-sheened darkness to be seen from the window. For a stomach-dropping second, the plane rolled in an air pocket then settled into the monotonous flight to Los Angeles.

Ellie settled in herself, knowing she would arrive in Los Angeles near dawn to change planes for the last leg to San Antonio. She closed her eyes, imagining Daniel at the cove.

He'd be there through the night, she knew, because it was what she would do herself. But in the morning where would he go?

To Nona's, she decided. Just as she would go to Gram's as soon as she arrived home.

There had to be a way of freeing Daniel permanently, and if Gram didn't know what it was, at least she would have some good ideas.

Fishing the silver plumeria out of her pocket, Ellie kissed it then out-stared the man beside her looking at her strangely. He snapped his attention back to his magazine.

With the earring clutched in her hand, she pulled the airline blanket up over her, turned her head toward the window and lulled herself to sleep composing letters of resignation.

Daniel awoke but remained unmoving for a long, disoriented moment. All was quiet. When a breeze passed over his damp body, he suppressed a shiver.

Where was he? Dead? In another lump of wood? Or in something else? Something worse?

Gritty damp pressed against the side of his face, and

it came to him that he lay on his belly in that same grit. He opened one eye and found the grit to be packed sand. His own outstretched arm filled his vision.

Tentatively his brain sent the command, and his arm, obeying, moved downward...revealing a silver plumeria half-covered with wet sand.

With a speed he didn't know he possessed, Daniel snatched the earring into his fist and tucked it protectively under his chest next to his heart.

He waited, senses fully alert now, for what might happen next.

Nothing did.

A bird called somewhere.

Cautiously Daniel sat up. Nothing held him. Nothing bound him. He was at the cove. It was just dawn.

The cove had rejected him, and it had rejected Ellie's earring. Opening his hand, he gazed at the silver flower in his palm. Oh, God. *Ellie.*

Anger rose, threatened to choke him, but found release instead in deep racking sobs. Standing shakily, he drew back his arm, and would have hurled the flower into the sea had some instinct not stopped him.

It was all he had now of a woman made of moonlight and giving.

With the earring clutched once more in his fist, Daniel turned toward the houses beyond. Chad probably wasn't at the apartment, but Nona would be home.

Nona embraced Daniel, clucking and crooning over his sodden state like a mother hen over a half-drowned chick, but she knew nothing of an airline crash. Nor was there anything on the news or in the newspapers.

Chad wasn't at the apartment. His unit left hours ago for Okinawa, Daniel learned. There was no way to contact him. The marine sub-leasing the apartment had no idea of Chad's, or Ellie's, home address. Nor had he heard of any airline disasters.

Whatever Daniel heard the night before was not the sound of an airplane in trouble. Probably his overactive imagination coupled with signs and portents meaning nothing, Daniel thought ruefully.

With the new tenant's permission, he showered and changed, then headed back to Nona's to discuss his new situation with her.

Deep in thought and halfway across the lawn, Daniel stopped midstride. Criminy! Had he no brain at all?

He'd showered. And without thinking, left the earring on the bathroom shelf as he did so.

He talked with the marine for a while in the living room, then returned to the bathroom for the earring he'd left there.

And all the while, without the earring in his hand or anywhere in his physical possession, he'd stayed put. A half-dozen times today he should have been zapped back into the tiki, but wasn't. Nor did he have the nausea and dizziness he'd experienced the night before.

Today, he felt...free.

He thought about that for a moment, then angled to the street leading to the cove.

Walking over the sand, he came to a stop at the water's edge.

Tiny waves rushed toward him, only to race back in their endless game of tag with the shell-strewn sand. The sea itself was a deep pure blue, the sun high overhead dusting it with gilt.

A light breeze plastered Daniel's shirt to his chest and ruffled his hair.

"Are you finished with me?" he asked the cove quietly.

The sea whispered the same song it murmured yesterday and the day before that and the eon before that. Daniel took it as a yes.

"You gave me Ellie," he said. "And you gave me the Kamehanas. You showed me what was important. Can't say I like your tough love, but I appreciate it. Now it's time I got my priorities in order. I'm going home."

The waves never changed their rhythm, the sea never changed its song. Daniel took it as a yes.

"He wasn't there, Gram. Daniel went home. Apparently he found a way to break the spell, but Nona didn't know how. He…he doesn't need me—I mean my earring—to be free anymore."

Ellie sat on the floor with her head on her grandmother's lap, just as she'd done when she was small. She felt Gram's hand brush over her hair.

There was comfort in the touch, but also the knowledge that healing came from oneself.

"And that's not a good thing?" Gram asked.

A good thing. Their own small joke, Ellie thought bleakly.

"Of course it's a good thing," she replied, trying to sound cross to cover the wave of loneliness threatening to swamp her—a loneliness she hadn't felt since the Kamehanas' luau. "It's just that, well, I'd thought we might be friends."

"It's not easy to be 'just friends' with the person you're in love with, Eliza Ann. Especially when you both chose different paths."

Ellie sighed, knowing exactly what her grandmother was getting at. "It's more than a choice," she replied firmly. "I promised LeAnne, Gram."

"And there's more than one way to keep a promise," Gram replied, her voice just as firm. "Now, darling, what are your plans for your next job?"

Chapter Twelve

He couldn't find her.

Ellie had said she worked for a pediatrician, and Daniel called every one listed in the San Antonio phone directory. None admitted having an Eliza Ann Simms working there. Then he called hospitals. No Ellie.

On the off chance she had a standard phone at home, as well as the cell phone he didn't know the number of, Daniel tried the San Antonio white pages. No luck.

No *Simms, Eliza Ann* at all, as a matter of fact, and the two *Simms, E.* politely told him he had a wrong number. Among the profanity used by the third, Daniel gathered the name was Eugene.

Determined, Daniel went back to pursuing the medical angle, working his way through every M.D. he found listed, from Aabidgen to Zyvenel, not caring what the specialty was, so long as they practiced medicine in San Antonio.

No Ellie Simms. No Eliza Ann Simms.

He'd been at it for two days, and now, blocked on all fronts, Daniel sat on the side of the bed in his hotel room and stared at the unhelpful phone.

Ellie was somewhere in this city and he'd find her if he had to knock on every door in San Antonio to do it.

But there had to be an easier way.

All right. What did he know?

Not much.

He knew Ellie had a married sister living in West Texas. He didn't know her last name. No help there.

He knew she had a brother, Chad. Definitely a Simms, according to the name tag on Chad's uniform. If he must, Daniel would use his own or his father's connections to track Chad down in Okinawa. That took time.

So what else?

He knew Ellie had a Grammie Simms. This time he didn't have a first name. He knew Gram lived in San Antonio...he sat up straight...and knew she was a physics professor at the university.

Jumael looked better. Not good, but better.

Ellie shooed away an ever-present fly and smiled down at the boy of about seven, who looked back at her with dull, heavy-lidded eyes. He took a few sips of the water she offered, then lay back, taking up a pitifully small amount of the cot serving as his hospital bed. While she checked his IV, then studied his chart, the child drifted back into sleep.

Not good. But better.

How many times had she said that to herself?

In a country recently ravaged by war, conditions in this African coastal village were already deplorable when cholera struck.

The IMO, recently arrived in the capital to aid in reorganization of medical facilities, hastily put together a team of doctors and nurses, loaded them unceremoniously into the back of a truck, and sent them on a two-day trip over near nonexistent roads to do what they could.

On arrival, it didn't take Ellie long to realize that nursing was only a small part of what was needed. Like everyone else on the team, she instantly became cook, dishwasher, carpenter and janitor. She dug ditches and collected water samples. At one point she even found herself bent over the innards of a truck trying to coax it into running again.

Eventually it did—not well, but better.

Now she passed down the line of cots, stopping at each to do what was necessary for the child in it. Some of her small patients, like their parents, were terribly sick, some now recovering, a few almost ready for release, and a few…

The numbers still weren't good, but they were better.

In spite of constant mopping, cleaning and disinfecting, the stench in the makeshift ward was overpowering. Ellie maneuvered yet another small charge so she could change the sheets under her.

"Let me help with that."

She froze.

It couldn't be. But, oh, the disappointment that it couldn't.

"I've got it," she said evenly, not looking up, and secured the sheet.

"Aloha, Ellie."

Two hands grasped her shoulders and gently turned Ellie around.

"Daniel!"

"Daniel," he said, and kissed her.

A weak laugh from the bed she'd just made brought Ellie to her senses. When she looked down, the little girl lying there was smiling. She whispered something in her own language, her big bright eyes alive with merriment.

Ellie couldn't help but smile back, but only for an instant. It was Daniel who claimed all her attention.

A ping of warning shot through her but she tamped it down. Not now. Not now.

She stared into his face unbelievingly. Then, unable to help herself, she reached to touch it, only to realize she still wore the latex gloves she used to change the sheets.

"What…I mean, how…Daniel, what are you *doing* here?"

He bussed her cheek but backed up a couple of steps.

"Gotta run," he said. "The what and how will have to wait, but what I'm *doing* right now…should be doing…is making rounds with Perkins, who's showing me the ropes. Catch you later." He grinned. "Plan on it."

Plan on it? *Plan on it!* Daniel wasn't in her plans, Ellie thought incredulously, watching him walk away, his stride quick and purposeful in a way she'd never seen it.

Months ago, when she flew back to Hawaii ready to save him, Nona told her he was free and gone home. Why hadn't he called?

But she knew why, even though it hurt unbearably.

The fiancée who waited and the Morgan dynasty that needed managing. Add Morgan babies to create and a flourishing clinic to give him something to do in the daytime.

So where was the fiancée, and who was tending the dynasty? Ellie wondered each time she had a spare minute to think. Which wasn't often.

She caught a glimpse of him on the roof of the building they were using as a hospital, but she was hurrying to conduct a women's nutrition meeting through an interpreter and didn't have time to stop.

Daniel waved his hammer when she passed but didn't stop what he was doing, either. None of the team had time for idle chitchat.

Well, whatever he was doing here, he better not have come for *her,* Ellie thought. He might have changed his mind about the focus of his life, but she hadn't.

Yes, she loved Daniel. And that kiss earlier said he still loved her. Big hairy deal. Didn't change a thing.

She had no time to be a wife, or anybody's partner, let alone a man's good little homemaker. She was a nurse. End of statement. And she'd promised.

Their paths finally crossed when Daniel stood at the makeshift sink scrubbing his hands and Ellie came up to wash hers, too.

"We have to talk," she said unceremoniously.

He grinned. A heartstoppingly carefree grin. The kind of grin Ellie never saw in Hawaii.

"I know," he said. "And I can hardly wait. But not now." He glanced at Perkins, standing a little way off and obviously waiting.

"I'm needed," he added. "Later, though." Giving her a quick peck on the cheek, he hurried off.

Later never seemed to come. When one of them had a few minutes of free time, the other was up to their back pockets in a job that wouldn't wait.

The day wore on. Ellie didn't have time to brood, but she had time to plan.

What she would say. How she would put her foot down. How she would let Daniel know in no uncertain terms that she didn't have time to be what he wanted her to be.

And he wanted, all right. It was written all over him every time he so much as glanced at her. When their gazes met and clung, the air still did its sizzle between them. She wanted, too. Just not everything Daniel did.

He thought in terms of dynasties. She thought…well, she didn't think past what she had to do tomorrow.

It was almost dark when Ellie finally looked around and realized everything she needed to do at the moment was done. She was exhausted.

There was still activity in the hospital but none of it needed her, though Daniel was probably still in the thick of it.

He must be exhausted, too, on this his first day.

There'd been no time to talk after all, she thought, and now she just wanted her hammock.

Gathering soap and her sponge bag, she headed for

the communal shower one of the doctors had rigged, feeling like a new woman when she emerged, clad in a loose-fitting flowered muu-muu.

A million stars spangled the African sky, rivaled only by a quarter moon. On impulse Ellie decided to walk down to the nearby beach.

She'd gone there several times since she'd been in the village. It reminded her of the cove, which reminded her of Daniel. Her memories were always bittersweet.

Tonight, however, Ellie wasn't thinking of Hawaii, or of the man she'd left behind there.

She was thinking of the man who was here, whom she knew had come to claim her.

Was she so weak that she could be claimed? Did her promise to LeAnne mean so little?

Loving Daniel was easy in Hawaii. The parameters of the situation had him bound by the tiki, and bound in a different way by his promise to a fiancée. Either of those things meant his love for Ellie, like her love for him, presented no real threat to the way Ellie saw her future.

But suddenly the future was now, and Ellie had a fight on her hands. Not with Daniel, but with herself.

As if conjured by her thoughts, Daniel stepped onto the beach to join her and wrapped her in his arms.

He smelled, she thought hazily, of soap and clean clothes, mixed with the faintest whiff of disinfectant.

The thought made her smile against his lips.

Pulling back, he looked at her inquiringly, his own smile bright in the moonlight. "What?"

"I love you," Ellie said, not what she'd planned to say at all.

"Oh, darlin', thank God for that. Sometimes I thought I might be only a really weird vacation romance for you. I love you, too, Ellie Simms Jenkins. Do you know what a time I've had finding you?"

Sore subject. "No, I don't. When I went back to Hawaii just two weeks after I left, you'd gone home, Nona said. You never called."

She would have pulled away, but he wouldn't let her.

"Ellie, I didn't have a number and I didn't have an address. But not having the right name was the biggest problem. All your listings are under your married name. I went looking for Ellie Simms, never dreaming I should be looking for Ellie Jenkins."

He sighed. "But I admit I went home first before I started looking. There were things I needed to take care of before I was free to do as I pleased."

Though Ellie allowed Daniel's loose embrace, she kept her posture stiff and unrelenting. "And did you take care of your fiancée?" she asked tartly.

"Well, no. It seems that Laura was no longer my fiancée, she was a wife."

When Ellie jerked, he laughed down at her. "Not mine. *She's* the happily married mother of two children with another on the way. No hard feelings, she hastened to assure me, even adding that she was glad I was alive."

But Daniel dropped his bantering tone when he continued, "She knew nothing about my mother's little prevarication. And Mother had no qualms about letting me know the story was simply a means of getting me home."

"I'm so sorry." Ellie nestled into his arms.

"Yes, well. It made it easier to tell her and my father

that I wasn't buying into the clinic after all. They were delighted, but when I said I wouldn't be taking an office in my father's building, either, they weren't quite so happy. I'm sorry for that, but there are other things I want to give my life to now. That's what the cove was wanting me to learn all along, but it took thinking I had lost you for me to realize it. Tracking you down took a while."

"Six months?"

"Three days. I flew to San Antonio but couldn't find you. I finally located your grammie, though, and she told me where you were. What took time was going through the application process to join the IMO, then getting the paperwork and so on together. Try explaining a four-year disappearance to International Security these days. Fortunately the Morgan name is good for something, and I used it freely to get posted to the back of beyond here."

He looked around. "Beautiful," he said. "Almost like our cove. Is the ocean safe?" but he smiled down at her to show he was joking.

Ellie wouldn't be diverted. "Grammie never told me. She could've written."

"I didn't get the impression your grammie ever does what she's supposed to," Daniel said, hiking an eyebrow.

And Ellie had to laugh. "No."

"I'll admit I'm glad. I wanted to surprise you." He rested his forehead against hers. "Did I?"

"Yes. But Daniel, I won't—"

"And before I got in touch with you, I wanted to make sure the IMO would accept me. I sure as hell wasn't going to make you have to choose. Ellie, what you're doing is so worthwhile, and I want to be part of it. But had the IMO not accepted me, you wouldn't have heard from me." He paused. "Except to tell you I was free."

His sudden grin was a small boy's who'd just found a shiny penny. "Lucky for me it did."

"But Daniel, I—"

"I know being married to a doctor is probably the world's toughest job," Daniel continued. "Would it bother you that I won't be able to dance attendance to you?"

"Of course not, but—"

"Though I definitely plan to dance *with* you," he said. "But I like the idea of practicing where I'm really needed. Would nursing under difficult circumstances be something you could handle?"

She laughed. "You're asking me that *here?* But, Daniel, I—"

"My heart is dedicated to you, Ellie, always. You have to know that. But, like yours, my medical skills are dedicated to my patients, even should I set up my own practice someday. Can you live with that?"

Defeated, Ellie bowed her head against Daniel's chest, silently conceding game, set and match. He'd just taken all her arguments and turned them inside out, mirroring them against her. The man was so darn slick. What could she say?

She lifted her head. "I'm a dedicated nurse," she said. "Can you live with that?"

Daniel kissed the silver dolphin pendant nestled between her breasts. "I can live with anything, so long as I can live with you. I think we make the perfect team."

"I think we do, too."

LeAnne, Ellie thought, as Daniel's mouth homed in on hers, *would be pleased.* Not only had Daniel not forced her to choose, he'd joined Ellie's promise to her daughter with a mission of his own, thereby doubling the vow.

A while later Daniel lifted his head so he could fish in his shirt pocket. He came up with Ellie's silver plumeria earring in his hand.

She laughed and pulled her hair back, showing him its twin in her ear. Daniel slipped his into the other one.

"There," he said. "Together again. I'll dance to your tune, if you'll dance to mine."

"Always." And Ellie's floated over the beach in Daniel's arms as he waltzed her to the song of sea, the same song it murmured yesterday and all the eons before.

But the waltz turned into a kiss, and the kiss led to their disappearance as hand in hand they left the beach to its music and returned to the village.

* * * * *